MURDER AS SAVORY AS BISCUITS

DIANA ORGAIN

Lemonade Press

OTHER TITLES BY DIANA ORGAIN

Third Time's a Crime If only love were as simple as murder…

<u>*Yappy Hour*</u> Things take a *ruff* turn at the Wine & Bark when Maggie Patterson takes charge

Trigger Yappy Salmonella poisoning strikes at the Wine & Bark.

<u>*A Witch Called Wanda*</u> Can a witch solve a murder mystery?

<u>*I Wanda put a spell on you*</u> When Wanda is kidnapped, Maeve might need a little magic.

<u>*Brewing up Murder*</u> A witch, a murder, a dog…no, wait…a man..no…two men, three witches and a cat?

Murder as Sticky as Jam Mona and Vicki are ready for the grand opening of Jammin' Honey until…their store goes up in smoke…

CHAPTER 1

*T*here was a spring in Leo Lawson's step as he walked the hay-bale-filled passageways of the Fall Festival at Magnolia Falls.

Today was the day.

He was finally going to ask Mona out. He'd known her since they were kids. Because she was his sister's best friend, he'd always figured their relationship couldn't ever be more than platonic. But the time had come. He couldn't stand the torment anymore. He had to ask her.

All around, the sights and sounds and smells of the Fall Festival tugged at him. Homemade pies. Locally brewed beer. Handcrafted furniture. The tangy scent of barbecue hit his nostrils, and his stomach rumbled. But no—he would not be lured away by Bandit Bob's BBQ or their fine pulled-pork sandwiches. He was a man on a mission.

He headed straight to the Jammin' Honey booth, where both Mona and his sister would be. Over the top of a hay bale, he spotted a colorful cowgirl hat that could only belong to Mona's eccentric Aunt Bee.

Abort! He couldn't do this with Aunt Bee here. She was wonderful, but she had a way of commandeering the room—and was never, ever shy about expressing her thoughts.

Leo spun on his heel to make a run for it, but Aunt Bee had spotted him.

She grabbed his elbow. She sure was fast on her feet for an octogenarian.

"Leo! I knew you'd make it. Have you had a chance to grab our latest coupon?"

Aunt Bee ran the local Coupon Clippers club, and she'd stop at nothing to get a great deal on a purchase.

"I've got the latest steal for you, hon," she said, squeezing his bicep as if she were juicing a lemon.

"What's that, Aunt Bee?" he asked, untangling himself from her grip.

"It's a two-for-one over at Greta Cox's beer booth." She gave him a direct look and waggled her eyebrows.

He laughed aloud. "That sounds great. Right up my alley. But I'm on duty."

"Well, save it for later," she said, turning her attention to the aisle, no doubt looking for her next catch.

Leo smiled despite himself and approached the Jammin' Honey booth. Vicki, his sister and the world's best purveyor of honeybee products, was chatting with some customers, but he didn't see Mona.

Where could she be? The anxious tug in his belly surprised him.

Vicki spotted him and waved him over. She finished chatting with her customer and then picked up a couple of packets and held them out toward Leo. "Got some samples for you."

He gave her a look. "Haven't I tried all your stuff before?"

Leo tended to be Vicki's guinea pig for all her body scrubs and face products. Some had turned out great, while others had been a little questionable. She'd once turned his face *green*.

Vicki laughed. "You can never have too many scrubs."

"I'm here to eat." Leo patted his abs and looked around. "Where's Mona?"

Vicki smirked at him. "Mona doesn't need to be here to feed you. Help yourself." She pointed toward the samples of homemade jams and jellies on the gluten-free bread Mona loved so much. Leo picked up a couple and stuffed them in his mouth.

"So . . . where is she?" he asked.

Vicki put her hands on her hips. "Aha! Are you finally going to ask her out?"

"I'd like to," Leo said. "And I'd like to do it without you being so nosy about it."

Vicki pumped her fist triumphantly. "You know I want my best friend to be my sister-in-law. Get to it."

"Well, where is she, for crying out loud?" Leo asked, exasperated.

"She'll be here soon. She was running over to talk to some of the people at the cheese booth to see if they could pair some dry cheeses with her jam."

Leo nodded. Mona was a workaholic. It was one of the things he liked about her. Before long, he glimpsed her honey-colored hair through the crowd, and a warm feeling filled his chest. A shy smile crossed Mona's face when she saw him, and the warm feeling grew.

"Hey!" Mona said. "Are you hungry? I've wrangled some cheese samples." She unpackaged the bundle she was carrying, and Leo dug into some cheese and grapes.

"Well . . . I had another reason for coming," he said after he swallowed. "Although this cheese is excellent."

Mona looked at him expectantly, and Vicki ducked down as if she were digging more product out of the boxes underneath the table.

He paused, then blurted, "I was wondering if maybe you had time Wednesday afternoon. I have the day off. I wanted to hike up to the falls, maybe have a picnic."

Mona bit her lip. "I'd love that," she said, her voice squeaking. "Wednesday it is."

They looked at each other awkwardly, and suddenly Leo didn't know what to do with himself. He wanted to kiss her, but that would be too much too fast. Like an idiot, he fought the impulse to stick his hand out to shake hers.

She'd agreed to a date, not a business deal, for crying out loud.

Clumsily, he stuck his hands in his pockets.

"I can pack the basket," Mona said, her cheeks reddening. "I'll get some more of these cheeses, and maybe a little wine?"

He nodded. "That sounds great." From his pocket, he fished out the

3

coupon Aunt Bee had given him and offered it to Mona. "Oh, I have a two-for. Two beers for the price of one, but I can't drink right now. I'm on duty." He tapped the police-issued radio strapped to his shoulder.

Mona accepted the coupon. "Thank you! Vicki and I will have some after we clean up our booth. We'll toast to you." She gave him a big wink, then seemed flustered about it. "It's . . . the last day of the festival. The booth has done really well, so it'll be good to have a way to celebrate."

"Good. I'm very glad," he said. "Now I need to go and patrol—keep this rowdy Fall Festival crowd under control."

As if on cue, a country band took the stage and started crooning a cover of "I Cross My Heart." In front of the stage, couples paired off to slow dance.

Leo and Mona exchanged looks. He wished he could stay and dance with her, but he needed to make the rounds. And it wasn't like he could ask her to slow dance yet; he'd just asked her on a first date!

Two teenage boys whizzed by them, a vendor in hot pursuit.

"Shoplifter!" yelled the vendor.

Adrenaline surged in Leo, and he bolted after the little thieves, shouting over his shoulder, "See you Wednesday!"

CHAPTER 2

*L*eo and Mona chatted happily as they climbed Magnolia Falls Trail. Mona had thrown her hair back in a ponytail and wore hiking boots, leggings that hugged her shapely form, and a long-sleeved workout tunic. Leo's heart pounded when he looked at her. Even in athletic clothes and without a stitch of makeup, she was so beautiful.

At the top of the trail, should he take her behind the waterfall and kiss her? People did that sort of thing in romantic movies. But this was only their first date. He didn't want to make her uncomfortable.

She tucked a loose strand of hair behind her ear and gave him a smile that made him dizzy. He took a step forward without thinking and almost tumbled off the side of the trail. He caught himself on a tree branch and glanced down at the ravine. He needed to pay better attention. A fall like that wouldn't kill him—it would be more of a long, inevitable roll than a sheer drop—but it would sure hurt.

And mortally wound his pride, no doubt.

Once they got to the top, they snapped a few selfies and texted them to Vicki, then set up their picnic on a long, flat rock near the roar of the waterfall.

Leo opened up the backpack and pulled out a blanket that Mona had packed. He laid it out, and they both plopped on top of it.

"I think I'm getting a blister," Mona said, taking off her shoes.

"Let me take a look," Leo said, grabbing for her foot.

She pulled back. "No way. My feet are sticky and gross."

"I don't care," he said, chuckling. "I did a tour in Afghanistan. I've seen sticky and gross feet before, believe me."

After a moment's hesitation, she let him look at her feet. He peeled off her sweaty sock and examined the back of her heel.

"Yup, you're working up a blister. Better air them out a little bit." Then he gave her a crooked grin. "I'd give you a foot massage, but your feet *are* kinda stinky and gross."

She kicked his legs with her bare feet. "Shut up, you big oaf. I'm sure your feet are way stinkier and grosser."

He kicked off his boots. "They're supposed to be. I'm an oaf."

He uncorked the bottle of wine and poured her a glass. Despite the late-autumn chill, the sun was warm in the sky, and the wine tasted a bit like heaven. He felt himself relax, starting from his shoulders. Mona was nervously chatting about the progress on the shop—her store had burned down a few months ago, and it was scheduled for its grand opening the day after Thanksgiving—but he was so intoxicated looking at her beautiful profile that he didn't really hear a word.

He scooched closer to her until their hips touched. He wrapped an arm around her waist, and she stiffened, suddenly going quiet. His breath hitched. Had he misread her signals? Did she not want him to touch her?

Mind racing, he released her. "I'm—"

A loud rustling in the bushes stopped him short.

Leo jumped to his feet as a golden retriever tore out of the brambles.

"What on earth!" Mona shrieked.

The dog wailed loudly and charged at them. Was that *blood* on its fur? Was it rabid? Had it been attacked by something?

Instinctively, Leo stepped between Mona and the dog. He regretted taking off his boots. Trouble never seemed to be far away; a string of bad luck seemed to have stalked the town of Magnolia Falls recently. The dog barked and whined mournfully.

"He's hurt," Mona said, moving toward the retriever.

"Hold up, hold up," Leo said. "Don't touch it."

The dog barked at them sharply, then tore off back into the woods. Leo and Mona glanced at each other. A moment later, the dog's snout poked through the bushes, and it barked again, as if beckoning them.

"He wants us to follow him," Mona said.

"You stay here," he told her, tying his laces.

"Not on your life," she said, sticking her feet into her boots. "I'm going with you."

"You're stubborn."

Mona snorted. "You like it."

He swallowed. She was right. And maybe her retort meant she *had* wanted him to put his arm around her?

She tore off after the dog, with Leo in hot pursuit.

The dog raced through the bushes, howling as it led them down a narrow path toward the bottom of the falls. A sickening pit opened up in Leo's stomach. This was trouble—he knew it. He grabbed for his shoulder radio and realized he hadn't brought it along. Of course he hadn't. It was his day off. He wasn't in uniform.

The dog galloped to the far side of a clearing. Once there, it stopped short and growled.

Leo reached for his ankle holster. Thank goodness some habits died hard, even when he was off duty in a small town.

"Stay here and call 911," Leo said to Mona. She pulled out her cell phone and dialed.

Leo reached the dog, now on point, and called out, "Police."

The silence was deafening. Then the dog began to cry. It whined and whimpered, finally laying its head on its forepaws.

"What is it, boy?" Leo asked. But somehow, he already knew.

He holstered his weapon and shoved aside the brush.

A body lay in the foliage—a man wearing a suit drenched in blood.

CHAPTER 3

"Not exactly the way I was hoping our first date would go," Mona said under her breath, looking anywhere except at the body in the brush.

Leo nodded, sighing heavily. He'd just gotten off the phone with dispatch, and they were sending a crime-scene unit. The dog whined, not budging from the man's side.

Yup, this year sure had brought a whole spree of bad luck to the town of Magnolia Falls. Their small community hadn't seen a murder in ten years, and then an arsonist had burned down Mona's store, killing someone in the process. Just a few months later, a pair of selfish siblings had murdered two people in a bid to keep themselves from being disinherited, and Leo's sister Vicki had been caught up in the middle of the investigation.

And now he'd found a body in the woods.

The dog pushed his nose into the man's face and whimpered mournfully.

"Come here, boy," Leo said, worried the dog was going to contaminate the crime scene. The dog whined again and limped over to Leo.

"Is he hurt?" Mona asked.

Leo bent down next to the retriever. Its face was covered in blood. From the dead man, maybe? The dog had been sniffing around him quite a bit. But upon further examination, he found a stab wound in the dog's front right leg.

"He's been stabbed," Leo said.

"The man?" Mona asked.

"The dog."

"You poor thing!" Mona cried, kneeling. The dog's tail thumped half-heartedly. While Mona fawned over the injured dog, Leo took another look at the body. What he saw chilled him to his core, and a protective instinct rushed over him.

"Oh my gosh! Mona, stay away from the dog!" he snapped, spinning around. The retriever was lying on its back, and Mona was rubbing its belly.

"Why?" she asked.

"This man . . . he was bit . . . in the throat . . ." Leo stood upright despite a wave of nausea.

Mona furrowed her eyebrows like he was crazy. "You think this sweet little guy killed him? There's no way."

"Mona, I don't know, but it kinda looks that way. Please, just back away from the dog."

She crossed her arms and stood up. "There's no way this dog killed that guy."

"Leo!" a voice called from beyond the trees.

"Over this way!" Leo called back, waving his arms as a handful of officers from the station's crime-scene unit trudged past the tree line.

"This dog is sweet," Mona insisted, still rubbing the retriever's belly. "If it hurt that man like that, it wasn't the aggressor. Maybe the guy was the one who stabbed him or something."

Leo eyed her, then turned and shook hands with his fellow officers and briefly explained how they'd come across the scene.

One of the younger officers, Reynolds, squinted toward the body. "Shoot, I know him."

"Who is he?" Leo asked.

"Jonathan Darsey," Reynolds said. "Business guy."

"I could have guessed that from the suit," Leo said.

"Oh, I know the name," said Officer Truff, the oldest member of the group. "He's new to town, isn't he?"

"Yeah," said Reynolds. "Well, sort of. He's from Pigeon Hollow originally. Lives somewhere in the county. I've heard it's a big estate, but I don't know where it is. But he just bought that big lot on the edge of town for his factory. What are they making? Boots or something?"

"Speaking of which," Mona said, stepping into the circle of officers. "What's a guy doing dressed like that in the middle of the woods?"

"Probably not hiking." Leo crossed his arms. "The dog does seem to know him, though."

"Doesn't take a genius to see that the dog bit him and that he bled out," Reynolds said. "Dog's gonna have to be put down."

"Don't jump to conclusions, rookie," replied Truff. "We're going to need an autopsy."

"Seriously?" Reynolds questioned. "The dog is covered in his blood, and that wound on his neck is obviously a bite mark."

Mona put her hands on her hips. "This dog didn't bite him!"

Reynolds shot a questioning look in her direction. "Unless the autopsy results show something crazy, it seems pretty straightforward to me."

"No, it doesn't," Mona retorted. "The guy's in the middle of the woods in a suit. No one walks their dog like that. Look at his shoes. It doesn't make sense. And someone even stabbed the poor dog in the leg."

"I don't know," Officer Truff said, his eyes kind. "If I had to guess, the dog attacked the victim, the victim stabbed back in self-defense, and its owner ran off when they realized their dog had killed the man."

Mona's hands shook, and she bit her lip like she might be about to burst into angry tears.

"Okay, let's slow down a bit, fellas," Leo said. "I think Mona might have a point. The scene is odd, and the dog hasn't shown any signs of aggression. Let's be sure we do a thorough sweep of the scene."

"What about the dog?" Reynolds asked.

"I guess we take it to the pound after we get a cast of its mouth to confirm whether or not it actually bit the victim," said Truff. "Then, after the autopsy, we'll know whether it needs to be put down or not."

Mona grabbed Leo's arm and shook her head, eyes wide. "They'll mistreat it," she whispered harshly. "They think it's a killer."

Leo sighed and glanced from Mona to the crime-scene unit to the retriever. He surprised himself with the next words out of his mouth. "I'll take the dog. It needs to be seen by a vet, and there's one near my house."

Reynolds stared at him, agape. "You're really going to watch this dog while this case is being investigated?"

"I don't see why not," Leo said. "I've got plenty of room, and my yard is fenced in."

Truff shrugged. "Let me check in with the chief and see if it's okay for the dog to come home with you, but he'll probably be glad he doesn't have to deal with the idiot who runs animal control. You three start on the crime scene, and I'll head back to the cruiser and radio the chief."

Leo looked down at the retriever. It was lying on the ground, head propped up on its front paws, occasionally letting out a soft whine.

Panic flared in Leo's chest. What had he just committed to?

Great going, Leo.

But then Mona threaded her fingers through his and squeezed his hand. A giddy smile flashed across his face.

This would be fine. This had been a *good* idea. If the dog was innocent, they couldn't very well let it be swept off to the pound. It might get euthanized prematurely there.

Mona sat next to the dog and rubbed its ears, murmuring in soothing tones. Though Leo kept a sharp eye on the retriever for any signs of aggression, it just lay there, its tail occasionally thumping from side to side.

A few minutes later, Officer Truff reappeared on the path, shooting Leo a thumbs-up. "You're good to take the dog," he called. "Just wait a few minutes for the forensics team. They need to swab the blood on the dog's fur and take a cast of its mouth."

When the forensics team arrived, they did their job quickly and efficiently, and the dog appeared no more aggressive even when three people were poking and prodding him and prying his mouth open to take the cast.

"See," Mona said quietly.

Leo couldn't help but agree with her. This wasn't a vicious dog. If it had attacked, it must have been severely provoked.

The dog willingly followed Mona down the trail, and she spread her picnic blanket across Leo's back seat and coaxed the dog into the car. He hoped the picnic blanket would be enough and that he wouldn't find bloodstains on his seats later, but he didn't breathe a word of that concern to Mona.

"Hey," he said as he made the first turn. "Can you call ahead and let the vet know we're coming?"

"Great idea!" She dialed, and after a brief conversation, she hung up and said, "They'll see us as soon as we get there."

Sure enough, they were ushered to an exam room as soon as they brought the dog in. The vet swept into the room, and Leo was struck by his gentle demeanor. But the vet cast a suspicious glance at Leo and Mona.

"I understand we have a stab wound?" the vet asked.

"That's right," said Mona. "On his front leg."

The vet bent down and scratched the dog's chin, then inspected the stab wound. "Blood on his fur too," he murmured. He looked up at Leo and Mona. "What happened?"

"We're not sure," said Leo. "I'm a detective. We found the dog at a crime scene, and I'm taking care of him while the case is under investigation."

The vet eyed Leo as if he didn't quite believe him, so Leo pulled out his badge and held it out for inspection. The vet studied it and nodded, then stood and stuck out his hand. "I'm Dr. Mansour. Pleased to meet you."

Leo returned the handshake.

Dr. Mansour looked back down at the retriever and said, "All right, big guy, should we get you up on the exam table?"

The dog's tail thumped.

Dr. Mansour and Mona eased the dog onto the table, and then Dr. Mansour gave the dog a shot to numb the pain.

The retriever hardly flinched.

"We're going to clean the wound and then stitch it up," Dr.

Mansour said. "He did really good with that shot. Are you a good boy?"

Leo and Mona sat while the vet finished treating the wound. When he finished, the dog raised its head and gave the vet kisses on his chin.

With a chuckle, Dr. Mansour said, "Really great dog. Some dogs I have to drug pretty heavily to get them to sit still for stitches, or even bring in a few techs to hold them down—or both. I've been bitten and knocked over I can't tell you how many times. A tech will be back in a moment with a couple days of pain medication. Make sure he doesn't overgroom the stitches, or we'll have to put a cone on him. Any questions?"

"Just one," said Leo. "So, nothing you've seen would make you think the dog has any aggressive tendencies?"

"Not at all. Why?"

"We're ruling him out as a suspect in a crime."

"Hmm." Dr. Mansour reached out and ruffled the retriever's ears. "What's the situation?"

"Dead guy," said Leo with a grimace.

Dr. Mansour's eyes widened. "With a dog bite?"

"It looked like there was a bite to the throat. Body was found in the woods. Dog led us to him."

Mona added, "The dog seemed sad."

Dr. Mansour nodded slowly. "Well, almost every dog can be pushed to violence in the right circumstances—just like almost any person can be. Some dogs will be violent if they feel threatened. Even more will be violent if their person is threatened. But if he led you to the body and seemed sad, I'd say with a fair degree of certainty that he's not your biter. I'd guess you'll discover that the victim was his owner." He reached out again and gave the retriever one more pat on the head. "Poor thing. Let me know if you need anything else, all right?"

"Thank you for all your help," said Mona.

Dr. Mansour nodded and left the room, leaving Leo alone with Mona and the dog.

"See?" Mona said with a self-satisfied look.

Leo sighed. "I agree with you. I really do. But you know what that scene looked like, and I don't want you to get too upset if they wind up putting him down."

Mona nodded slowly. "I understand. But those other officers just seemed so quick to jump to conclusions."

"You know, I didn't see a knife on Darsey," Leo said. "Which probably means someone else was at that crime scene. It's possible the knife will be found by the other officers. I didn't have much of a chance to look around, because we left before they finished processing the evidence. But if Darsey stabbed the dog, it's going to come off looking like he was trying to defend himself against a mauling."

Mona sighed. "It just doesn't feel right, Leo. I mean, I'm a big animal person, I know. So I'm sure it seems like I'm biased. But just look at him."

Leo glanced down at the retriever that was now curled up on the floor, looking impossibly dejected.

"Plus," said Mona. "He's a golden retriever. They're family-friendly dogs. I've never met an aggressive one."

That was a fair point. Had Leo seen a single biting incident in a golden retriever in his time on the force? He didn't think so.

A vet tech returned, handing Leo a bag. "The meds will help the poor guy with pain," he said. "Wrap one pill up into some bologna or ham to get him to eat it. Once in the morning and once at night. Give him the first one tonight before you go to bed, and he should be okay. You're going to want to be careful when bathing him too. His stitches are fine to get wet, but you'll want to be very gentle around the wound."

Leo nodded. "Yeah, he's going to need a bath, for sure."

"Last thing." The tech held up a wand of some kind. "Mind if I scan him for a microchip? See if we can track down the owner that way?"

"Please do," said Leo.

The tech waved the wand over the dog's neck and shoulders. "We've got a chip!" he exclaimed. "I'll call the chip company and get you the owner's information."

At checkout, Leo cringed at the six-hundred-dollar bill. Maybe the station would reimburse him, but he doubted it. He'd volunteered to take care of the dog, so he was probably going to be stuck with the bill. He sighed and handed his credit card to the receptionist.

"Good boy. Who's a good boy? Who's a good boy?" crooned Mona behind him. He glanced over his shoulder. She was kneeling down on the floor, scratching the dog behind the ears. The dog's tail was wagging as it rubbed its head against her arms.

"That poor thing," the receptionist said as she ran Leo's card. "Why would someone hurt such a sweet dog?"

Leo shrugged. He was still thinking about the massive credit card bill he was going to have to pay at the end of the month.

Then the vet tech came into the room, frowning. "So, the dog is chipped, but the company said that there's no owner information—that the owner called in last Friday asking for all their information to be taken off the chip's record. They weren't able to give me more than that."

Last Friday? Leo frowned. Odd. That was before the time of death. Even if the owner had planned to sic the dog on Jonathan, surely they hadn't planned on leaving it out in the woods as evidence.

He and Mona headed out, and the dog walked right at their heels. It didn't even need a leash.

Leo dropped Mona off at her house, and she smiled brightly at him before she climbed out of the car and headed toward her door. When she was safely in the house, he let out a long sigh. The dog gingerly picked its way over the console and into the passenger seat.

Leo absentmindedly reached out and scratched the retriever's head.

What in the world did I get myself into?

CHAPTER 4

When Leo pulled into his driveway, he checked his phone and found a text message from Maxine, an officer on the station's forensics team.

Blood on dog's face matches victim, she'd written.

Leo rolled his eyes. Of course the blood belonged to Darsey. The dog had been sniffing around the body and setting his head on the man's chest. That didn't mean the dog had bitten the guy, right?

Then he sighed. A dog wasn't presumed innocent until proven guilty, and things weren't looking great. He hated the idea of telling Mona they were going to put the dog down.

Hopefully it wouldn't come to that.

The retriever looked out the window curiously, as though critically observing the front yard to get a feel for where he'd be staying.

"All right, boy, if you're going to sleep in my house, we're going to have to get you cleaned up," Leo said, climbing out of his car and walking around to the passenger-side door. The dog stumbled out of the car like a drunk college kid. "Geez, those meds they gave you are pretty strong, huh?"

The dog ambled lopsidedly, like he couldn't see straight.

Leo shook his head. "At this rate, it'll be midnight before you make it through the front door." He knelt by the dog, a little hesitant. He didn't *think* the dog had killed Jonathan Darsey, but he didn't *know* that. Last thing he wanted was for the thing to get irritated and bite him in the face. He touched it gently.

"Gonna pick you up, okay, boy?" he said, scooping it up very slowly.

The retriever licked his cheek.

Leo cringed. "All right, that's enough."

He brought the dog to his guest bathroom and ran water in the tub. After some convincing, he was able to coax the dog in. He didn't have dog shampoo, so he hoped his own shampoo would be good enough.

As he lathered up the dog, his phone buzzed. It was Maxine from forensics again. *No evidence in dog's mouth that it bit anyone recently.*

"Looks like Mona might have been right about you," Leo said to the exhausted dog. The phone buzzed with one more text from Maxine.

We'll know whether the bite marks match the dog's teeth soon. Chief says to keep him locked up at your place or on a leash at all times until we know. Chief thinks you should probably put a muzzle on him too—up to you.

Leo looked at the retriever. "Do you need a muzzle?" he asked, and the dog whined. He smirked. "I think that might be overkill."

He was *definitely* starting to side with Mona on this one. By the time they finished the bath, the dog was acting a little less doped up. At least he was walking straighter.

Leo slumped on the couch and turned on an old sitcom rerun while the dog sniffed around. The next thing he knew, it was sitting next to his leg, holding some slippers in its mouth.

"Where did you even find those old things?" Leo took the shoes and patted the retriever's head. "Um . . . good boy."

The dog limped off. Leo set the slippers under the coffee table and propped his feet up. He heard a whine and looked over. The dog was sitting up straight in the same spot, this time holding a pair of sweatpants in its mouth. It wagged its tail and inched forward, as if it wanted Leo to take the pants.

"Thanks," Leo said, chuckling and setting the sweatpants on top of the slippers.

Was this some sort of doggie scavenger hunt?

Sure enough, about ten minutes later, the dog brought him a candle from the table near his front door.

"Why do you think I need a candle?" Leo asked. "You're a weird fella, aren't you?"

He took the candle, and off the dog went again.

Leo snorted and shot off a series of texts to his sister about the dog. Vicki was more of a duck person than a dog person, but she'd definitely find the strange fetch game entertaining.

As the evening wore on, the dog brought him a picture frame, another pair of shoes, a book, a throw pillow, three magazines, and six pairs of socks.

"I get the feeling you're wanting some attention?" he asked when the dog arrived with the toilet plunger. Leo returned the plunger to the bathroom, shaking his head. *I'm going to have to close all the doors in the house, or he'll keep cleaning out all my rooms.*

Leo wandered around the house closing doors, eventually returning to the living room, where he gathered the things the dog had fetched—but not before taking a picture of the giant pile of random household items to send to Vicki. And maybe to Mona too.

The dog followed him into the kitchen and started whining.

"You hungry, boy?" Leo asked.

The dog's ears perked straight up.

"Hmmm . . . I probably should have gotten some dog food before coming home. I can pick some up for you tomorrow, but I guess you get leftovers tonight."

He opened up his fridge: two Tupperwares of leftovers, an apple, and a carton with four eggs.

"Geez," Leo grunted. But he grabbed the Tupperware full of chopped steak. "Lucky dog. You better not get used to this, all right? I'm definitely not feeding you steak every night."

He set the Tupperware down in front of the dog. "All right. Eat up, buddy."

The dog sniffed at the plate and walked away.

"Seriously? That was steak! What kind of dog doesn't like steak?" he demanded. Then he glanced down at the container and wrinkled his nose in disgust. "Hey! You drooled in the bowl! Now it's just a waste!"

With a sigh, Leo decided to leave the bowl sitting out in case the dog changed its mind. He also set out a water bowl, but the retriever seemed uninterested in the water as well.

Should he be concerned? He glanced at the clock. The vet's office was definitely closed. Likely the dog was still feeling the effects of the medication or the traumatic day.

Leo headed upstairs and took a quick shower before changing into some sweatpants and plopping into bed. Downstairs, the dog's claws click-clacked against his hardwood floor. It sounded like the poor thing was pacing—probably frightened to be in an unfamiliar place.

Poor thing? Now he sounded like Mona.

His phone buzzed, and he grabbed it from his nightstand to see a message from Vicki.

I CANNOT BELIEVE your first date with Mona turned into a crime scene!! We have the worst luck! Exciting about the dog though. You going to keep him? Also, stop by tomorrow before you head into work?

Leo texted back, *I can't believe it either. I'm not planning on keeping him—I'm sure we can find his owner or find him a good home once his name is cleared. Sure, I can come by tomorrow morning.*

He lay back down and tossed and turned for fifteen minutes. But his mind was racing at a million miles an hour. There was no point in trying to go to sleep.

Maybe just a little preliminary research on Jonathan Darsey. He grabbed his laptop. The very first thing that popped up was an article about the new factory. He skimmed it. Ground was scheduled to be broken next week. It would bring a lot of new jobs to Magnolia Falls. A brief overview of Darsey's past business ventures. Apparently, the man had revitalized a number of small towns in the area with his factories.

"So far, so good," he mused.

The second piece he read, however, wasn't quite so glowing.

Darsey Industrial Settles Pollution Case.

Apparently, a couple of other Darsey factories had dumped massive amounts of waste in nearby rivers, contaminating groundwater and making kids sick—although it looked like Darsey didn't own those factories anymore. A local environmental group—a chapter of Go Green—had taken up the fight against the new factory that was being built in Magnolia Falls. Leo's eyes were starting to droop, so he flagged the article to come back to it later. He yawned, put away his laptop, and turned off his bedside lamp.

Almost as soon as his head hit the pillow, a soft whine jolted him wide awake. He opened his eyes.

The dog was standing right by his head, staring at him. Leo sat up, startled, and then chuckled. The retriever was doing what looked to be the doggie version of a toddler's potty dance.

"Of course . . . you have to go out," he groaned, throwing his feet over the side of the bed. His feet landed perfectly in some slippers that hadn't been there before. He jumped in surprise. Then he looked down at the retriever.

"Smart dog," he said, rubbing his eyes. "Ugh . . . I gotta get you a leash too. Chief wants me to keep you on a leash outside. But the backyard's fenced, so you won't need a leash there, at least."

Leo walked the dog into the backyard, shivering at the sharp chill in the nighttime air. The dog did his business, and Leo called him back in. "Time for bed," he declared.

He was just entering a deep sleep when the mattress shifted and the distinct smell of dog breath hit his nostrils. He flipped on his lamp and found the dog lying right next to him.

"Oh, no! No, you don't! Not on my furniture, and especially not on my bed!" He shooed the retriever away and walked him back down into the kitchen. "You're lucky I'm letting you stay inside. Now, stay. Stay here. Sleep here."

Leo headed back to his bedroom and made certain the door was closed before climbing back into bed. Just as he was entering the halfway place between wakefulness and dreams, the mattress shifted again.

"No way," he said under his breath, flipping the light back on. "How!" He glanced toward the bedroom door that now stood wide open. The dog whined sadly and scooted closer to him.

"Up! Up, now!" Leo demanded, shoving the dog off the bed. The dog curled up in a corner of the room. "No—kitchen!" Leo said, pointing out the door.

The dog flopped over onto its back, its tongue lolling out. Leo rubbed his temples. He stalked over to the bedroom door, trying to figure out how the dog had managed to open it.

"Can you . . . open doors?" he asked in exasperation.

But a moment's investigation revealed that the door popped open if he pushed on it hard enough. "Great," he said. "So just this door." He turned around.

The dog had snuck over to his bed and was making himself at home.

"Hey! You're on my pillow!"

The dog sprawled out, clearly intent on resisting his command. Leo glanced at the clock. It was nearly two a.m., and he had to get up early now that he'd promised his sister he would stop by before work.

"Okay, fine. You win. You can sleep in the bed." He came over and gave the dog a slight shove so he could squeeze in beside him. He pointed a finger. "Don't you dare get used to this," he warned.

The dog licked his face, and a chuckle escaped Leo.

"You're welcome." He reached over and turned off the lamp before lying down. The dog rested his head on Leo's stomach. Despite the frustrating evening, a sense of affection and protectiveness welled up in Leo.

He wouldn't let them kill this dog. He couldn't.

CHAPTER 5

*L*eo awoke to the horrible smell of dog breath. He opened his eyes slowly. The retriever was lying with its head right next to Leo's and . . . was that *dog drool* on his pillow?

"Ack!" Leo yelped, sitting up. The dog sat up as well, shaking its tail and giving him a big, sloppy kiss across the face. Leo headed into the kitchen, the dog right on his heels as he fixed himself a pot of coffee. The steak still sat untouched in the Tupperware on the floor.

"What's your problem?" he asked. "I mean, what kind of dog doesn't love meat? Do I need to call the vet?"

The dog whined and lay down on the wood floor.

"I'll see if Vick can pick you up some dog food. Maybe your owner just didn't like you eating table scraps or something? Well, come on, boy. Let's go outside so you can do your business."

When Leo prepared to leave the house for the day, the retriever cried and lay in front of the door as if to keep Leo from going.

"Sorry, buddy, but I got to get to work."

The dog's whine faded to a pathetic little whimper.

"Aww, come on, don't guilt-trip me. If it weren't for me, you'd be at the pound right about now."

The retriever was still whining when Leo closed the door behind him.

He felt guilty leaving, but it wasn't as if he had a choice. He wished he could let the dog run around in the yard while he was gone, but if it escaped, the chief would have Leo's head. "All right," he muttered as he climbed in his car. "Next stop, Vicki's."

The familiar sound of buzzing bees greeted him as he walked up to Vicki's door. Vicki had a very successful backyard beehive that provided all the honey and beeswax she needed for her business. If he were a betting man, he'd wager she'd invited him over to sample a new product.

So long as it's not a face mask or scrub, he thought. In his latest stint as her guinea pig, a cranberry scrub had left his arm covered in pink blotches. He rang the doorbell, and a frantic, familiar quack started up in the backyard.

"Hey, DuckTales!" he called. "Just me."

The quack belonged to Vicki's pet duck, Sunny. His sister admittedly had eccentric taste in pets. But that was just the way she was.

The door flew open, and Vicki ushered him in. "So, how was it? Besides the murdery part? Was the picnic nice? Did Mona have fun? Do you have another date planned anytime soon?"

Leo laughed. So maybe she didn't want him to be a guinea pig—she just wanted him to dish out more details about the date. "It went . . . it went well. Until the *murdery part*."

"Mona said the police think the dog might have hurt the guy?"

"Oh, so you've already grilled Mona about the date?" He furrowed his brows. "Why are you interrogating me, then?"

She rolled her eyes dramatically. "I want to get *your* perspective, obviously."

"Well, what's Mona's perspective?" he asked. Why did his face feel so warm?

She grinned at him. "My lips are sealed," she said. "*Buuuut*, I will say that I'm pretty sure she'll say *yes* if you ask her on a second date."

He couldn't hide his grin, so he changed the subject. "Um, yeah, the victim had what looked like a bite out of his throat. Pretty bad. A couple of the responding officers thought the dog might have done it."

"What do *you* think?" asked Vicki.

Leo shrugged. "He's a nice dog. Mona didn't think he was capable of hurting someone, and I'm inclined to agree. Although the vet did say that most dogs can be pushed to violence, especially if their person is threatened. I think it might be the victim's dog though. Seemed pretty sad about the whole thing."

"Poor thing sounds traumatized!" Vicki cried.

"Something like that. He wouldn't go to sleep last night until I let him into bed with me."

"You let the dog sleep in bed with you?" Vicki asked. "Aww, you *are* a softy, huh?"

He waved his hand. "Whatever makes you feel better, Vick. So, did you just invite me over this morning to talk about my disaster date with Mona, or do you have something more diabolical in mind?"

Vicki laughed. "No body scrubs this time, I swear. I want you to tell me what you think about my honey spoons." She pulled some lollipop-looking things out of the fridge. He looked more closely. They were thin wooden spoons coated with a honey-flavored candy. Then she poured some tea and placed the spoons into the mugs. "I can't decide if the honey taste is too strong."

"Herbal tea with honey," Leo said. "That sounds safe. Not at all like the body scrub incident."

She laughed, and the two of them stirred their spoons into the tea. Once the honey treats had melted, they sipped the tea, and a perfectly smooth blend of sweetness filled his mouth.

"Ooh, that's good," he said. "Like, really good."

"Not too sweet?"

"Spot on! How'd the festival go, by the way?"

"Sales were great!" said Vicki. "And my online store is still doing well after the feature on Alana's blog. The business is . . . working, somehow. Against all odds."

"And things are still going all right with James?" he asked. A huge grin lit up her face, and he chuckled. "That smile says it all. I'm glad. You two make a cute couple."

They sat in companionable silence for another few moments, then Leo stood. "Well, I probably should head off to work. But I'm taking the rest of this tea with me, if you don't mind pouring it into a thermos."

"Glad it's good enough to take more for the road!" Vicki exclaimed, jumping up to pour more tea and pass another honey spoon his way. "Okay, last order of business before you go . . ."

"There's more?"

She handed him the thermos. "You need to ask Mona out again. And soon."

Leo laughed. "Isn't that up to me?"

"Nope!" she said cheerily, crossing her arms. "You two are meant to be. I'm telling you."

"You just like the idea of your best friend marrying your brother. And I'll have you know that it's weird to already be in that mindset, seeing as we've only been on one date . . . half a date, even. Because I don't think taking a canine murder suspect to the vet counts as part of the date. But yes, I'll ask her out again. And I'm sure it'll go better this time. It's not like we weren't having fun before we, you know, stumbled across a dead body."

Vicki shook her head. "See, now that's what I'm talking about. You and Mona are both disasters waiting to happen. I'm going to have to intervene."

"Excuse me?"

"I'm going to make sure the next date goes well," she said. "I'm planning it."

Leo shook his head. "There's no way I'm letting you plan my next date."

"You like her?"

"Of course I do."

"Then all the more reason to let her best friend help you out," she argued. "I know Mona better than anyone. If anyone can plan a perfect date for her, it's me. And there's no one who wants you two to wind up together more than me."

There would be no talking her out of it, and she *did* have a point. He held up his hands. "I surrender. By the way, the dog wouldn't eat my steak leftovers last night. I'm going to have a full shift at work today investigating the Darsey case. Would you mind picking up some kibble for him? Maybe you could head over there around lunchtime so you can let him into the backyard for a few minutes? Oh, and I couldn't get him to take his pain meds last night or this morning, either, since he wouldn't eat. So maybe mix one of those in the kibble? They're on the counter."

"Of course." She nodded and tapped her chin as she often did when deep in thought. "Anything to relieve you of some stress so that you can focus on what's important."

"The case?"

She threw her hands out in exasperation. "Mona, you dope!"

CHAPTER 6

Leo stepped out of his squad car, eager to start work. To do something that felt *normal*. Police work was his normal. Housing the world's politest murder suspect? Not so normal. Waking up to dog drool on his pillow? *Definitely* not normal.

Solve the Darsey case. Save the darn dog. Ask Mona out.

He could do this.

But his positive attitude was cut short when he spotted a familiar face in the midst of a group of officers.

Larry Simmons.

Or, as Leo liked to call him, Larry Simpleton Simmons. He couldn't stand the guy. He was brash and arrogant and a notorious ladies' man. It didn't help that Larry had long been in pursuit of Mona.

But Leo had thought he'd finally seen the last of him; over the summer, Larry had been hired by the Boston Police Department and moved to Massachusetts. So, what was he doing here? Or, more pertinently, what was he doing here wearing a Magnolia Falls PD uniform?

"So, there I was," Larry said to the other officers. "Three guys surrounding me. One of them was armed." He held up his hands as though grasping an invisible gun. "Pop. Take out their shooter first, lower my gun for the unarmed bunch. They come at me, and I manage to sock one of them with the back of my pistol. He fumbles back into the third guy, and I kick his stomach, knocking them both down. I point my gun—" The man paused, glancing in Leo's direction. "Well, if it isn't my old buddy, Leo. Was wondering if you were ever going to make it in."

Leo frowned. He was only ninety seconds late. "I had some stuff to take care of this morning. What are you even doing here? Thought you'd gotten yourself a job in the big city."

"I did, and it went really well," Larry said. "But I put in for a transfer. Family stuff. It was too bad, though. Boston is pretty exciting compared to this one-horse town."

"Uh-huh." Leo shook his head, pushing past the other officers who were gawking at Larry. The last person Leo had expected to see was big-shot Larry Simmons. The man had become sort of a local celebrity thanks to his degree from Harvard. Personally, Leo had always thought the guy had a big head. Like he thought he was better than everyone else.

But Leo wasn't going to let Larry's presence deter him from getting right to work. He was on a mission. Step one: find the dog's owner. Step two: see who might be especially motivated to hurt Darsey. His mind churned on the unanswered questions. Had the medical examiner finished the autopsy? What on earth had Darsey been doing so far away from civilization dressed in a suit?

Leo found a wrapped gift sitting on his desk. He stared at it, glancing around his cubicle to see if anyone was looking his way. He turned on his computer, then picked up the package. From the shape and feel, it was definitely a framed photograph. A little slip of paper across the top said, *Enjoyed our date! –Mona.*

A smile crept across Leo's face. He carefully unwrapped the gift—a picture of him and Mona near the waterfall. It must have been one of the selfies they'd taken.

"Well, I'll be," he said, setting the picture frame on his desk. *Guess the date wasn't a total disaster.* Then he spotted a jar of jam and a box of gluten-free crackers. Strawberry jam! His favorite. He opened the jar and dipped a cracker in the jam.

A voice behind him said, "Whoa, is that Mona?"

Leo nearly choked on the cracker. He spun in his chair to see Larry standing in the entry to the cubicle, arms crossed.

Larry whistled. "Man, she is as gorgeous as ever," he said, leaning over Leo's desk and picking up the photo. "That's cute. Wait, you two dating or something?"

"We went on a date," he said, snatching the picture back. "So . . . you requested a transfer for family reasons?"

"Yeah," Larry said. "Put in for it Tuesday morning, actually. Was surprised it came in so quickly. Just some family drama, really. They can't seem to stay sane without me. I have that effect on people. Once people get a taste of Larry Simmons, they've just got to have him around to function. Mona knows." He winked.

"I know you two never dated, Larry," Leo said. "Don't be a creep."

"Maybe we did, maybe we didn't. How is she, anyway? She's still making those jams, I see."

"Yeah," Leo said. "She's been rebuilding the shop after the fire, and it should open soon."

"Impressive. I should totally pop in. Catch up."

Leo rolled his eyes. "Do what you want. Look, Simmons, I've got a lot of work to do."

"Yeah, I heard," Larry said with a smirk. "Heard you were dog-sitting for the department now. My cousin has a Shih Tzu. How much you charge to walk 'em?" He laughed loudly.

"Ha," Leo grumbled. "Mind giving me some space? I really do have a lot of work to do."

"Ooooh . . . I get it . . ." Larry said. "Chief hasn't told you yet."

"Told me what?"

"I'm helping you out on the Darsey case!"

Leo's stomach churned. He stood upright. "No, Ann's my partner. She and I will handle it."

Larry shrugged. "Don't know what to tell you, but the chief's having Ann run point on a string of burglaries down on Alder Street. You and I have the Darsey case."

"Excuse me for a minute." Leo stalked past Larry and headed toward the elevator.

The chief looked briefly startled when Leo stormed into his office but quickly recovered himself. "Good to see you, Lawson. Glad that dog left you in one piece."

"Please tell me Larry's messing with me. You don't seriously want us working together on the Darsey case?" To be on the safe side, he added, "Sir."

"As a matter of fact, I do." The chief threaded his fingers together. "With a victim like Jonathan Darsey, it's a high-profile situation. Putting the local poster child on the case will make the citizens of Magnolia Falls feel like we're on top of things. Besides, as soon as Simmons got wind of the fact that we have some real detective work on our hands, he wanted a piece of the action. Even during his short time in Boston, he got a lot of experience working homicides."

"And my presence is inadequate? *Ann's* presence would be inadequate?"

"You know that's not what I meant," the chief said with a wave of his hand. "I just mean that Simmons brings a certain confidence—"

"You mean arrogance," Leo grumbled.

The chief slammed his fist on his desk. "Lawson, I swear, don't make this harder than it has to be. You and Simmons are working together on this one. And I'd be careful with that mouth of yours. Simmons has more experience than you. He comes from Harvard. How many Harvard boys come back to serve as police officers in their small hometowns? If anyone's expendable, it's going to be you."

Leo grimaced. "Understood, sir."

"You keeping that dog on a leash?"

"Who, Larry?" Leo said with a smirk.

The chief trained a glare on him.

Leo did his best to look apologetic. "Yes, sir. But I'm starting to think Mona has a point. After spending an evening with the dog and consulting with the veterinarian, I seriously doubt him bit Darsey. It's well behaved. Trained."

Well, mostly well behaved. Entirely too insistent on sleeping in my bed.

"Get with forensics about the cause of death. You never know what they'll find," the chief said. "Now, get out of my office and go make nice with your new partner. You know, most of the officers here would kill to be partnered with Simmons."

"Whatever you say, sir."

Leo shook his head and slowly made his way downstairs. Halfway to his cubicle, he caught sight of Larry dazzling the two rookies on the force.

"So," Larry said, "just like that, I wound up nabbing four out of the five guys in one night. The last guy was so freaked out after the story aired locally that he turned himself in!"

One of the rookies exclaimed, "Heck yeah!"

Leo wanted to puke.

"Larry, my desk!" Leo yelled.

Larry laughed and followed him into the cubicle, hopping up to sit on his desk.

"So, looks like you and I are stuck working together," said Leo.

"I told you. Chief thinks you could benefit from my help."

"Yes, I'm sure that's exactly what he said," Leo muttered. "Give me some space, would you?"

"Whatever you need, partner. I'm going to grab myself another cup of joe. You want any?"

"I'm good," Leo said. "I just need a minute, all right?"

Once Larry trotted off to the break room, Leo felt like he could breathe again. He rubbed his forehead. This was shaping up to be a very long week.

"Rough morning?" a feminine voice asked.

He looked up to see Ann Kimura, his now ex-partner, grinning at him.

"You could say that," he replied, his mood momentarily improving. Ann was one of the most competent officers he'd ever known, and her sense of humor made her fun to work with.

He couldn't believe she'd been swapped out for Larry Simmons.

"Is it the four-legged dog or the two-legged one?" she asked, nodding toward the break room.

Leo laughed wryly. "Glad to see that someone around here sees through that facade of his."

She rolled her eyes. "He's full of it. He wasn't gone long enough to have all those stories he's telling. He was still a rookie in Boston. He probably came back because he was a big joke out that way."

"No wonder you're the best partner I've ever had."

"I know I'd be using up my sick days if I got stuck working with him," she said, tucking back a strand of dark hair that had escaped her bun. "He'd give anyone a week of migraines. So, what's the deal with the Darsey case? You found the body when you were off duty?"

Leo grunted. "Mona and I were on our first date."

"Hey!" She grinned and slugged him in the arm. "You asked her out finally?"

"Yeah," he said. "And then our first date turned into a crime scene."

Ann pursed her lips sympathetically and nodded for him to continue.

"Mona got pretty upset over the dog," he said. "I feel a little obligated to prove that the dog didn't hurt Darsey. Besides, I kept him last night, and it's really nice."

"Oh, you don't think the dog did it? Heard there was a clear bite mark."

"There is," said Leo. "But there's more than one dog in the world. And we found him in the woods, so it's not like there aren't other animals out there."

Ann squinted at him. "Not much out there, unless you think some privately owned exotic animal got loose or something."

"Coyotes?" Leo asked.

She shook her head. "They don't attack full-grown adults. I think there's been one adult coyote fatality in North America, like . . . ever."

"Mountain lion?"

"They're extinct here."

"Bear?" he asked, throwing his hands out.

She shook her head. "We only have black bears. They very rarely attack—usually only when they're starving. I don't think there'd be any risk of confusing a black bear kill with a dog kill."

He sighed. "I know, I know. I don't think it's a wild animal, either, to tell you the truth. There's something funny about the case. It doesn't feel quite right. I'm going to get to the bottom of it though."

"I know you will."

"Hey, partner!" Larry called as he made his way back from the break room, a mug of coffee in his hand. "Oh, and if it isn't the always-lovely Ann!"

Ann rolled her eyes, then gave Leo a wink and mouthed, "Good luck."

CHAPTER 7

*L*eo couldn't remember a time when he'd been more miserable at work. Larry had been unbearable. Constantly breathing down his neck, asking stupid questions, and acting condescending at every turn.

Not to mention his constant questioning about Mona. It was no secret that Larry had had a thing for Mona back in the day, but to blatantly ignore the fact that Leo was clearly seeing her was beyond egoistical even from a big-headed city cop. And the way most of the other cops had fawned over him the whole day had made Leo want to puke. He breathed a sigh of relief when the clock struck five.

When Leo got home, the dog came running up to him, tail wagging. He bent over, and the retriever greeted him with a hundred kisses straight to the face.

"Eww," exclaimed Leo, pulling back—even though he couldn't help but laugh.

The dog jumped back, whining, then started doing its skippy dance. "Time to go out again?" asked Leo. "Good thing Vick came by or there might be a puddle on the floor."

When the dog came trotting back into the house, Leo glanced at a full bowl of kibble on the kitchen floor. It appeared untouched. He called the dog over and pointed down at the food bowl. "Come on, you need to eat something."

But the retriever didn't seem the least bit interested.

Leo sighed and whipped out his cell phone to call the vet. But a chipper voicemail greeted him, letting him know they'd closed at five and urging him to leave a detailed message after the beep.

Instead, he hung up and decided to call back tomorrow.

The retriever reached up to lick his hand, and Leo smiled down at him. "Good boy," he murmured. "Hey, I forgot the case file in the car. I should go get that, huh?"

When he returned, he kicked off his shoes and flopped down on the couch. "Do you want to help me solve this case?"

The dog planted himself in front of the couch, gently wagging his tail.

"You look like you've made yourself comfortable," he said, opening up the file he and Larry had put together.

Not that Larry did much of the actual work.

Leo had created a sort of web of people Jonathan Darsey knew, starting with his ex-wife. From what he'd found, it sounded like the divorce had been dramatic, with a number of nasty court battles and off-the-record mediation sessions. He'd requested court transcripts, but social media postings alone attested to the hard feelings.

Then there was the leader of the local Go Green chapter. He'd been actively organizing protests against the new factory, one of which had gotten rowdy when a group had flipped a Darsey Industrial truck. He ran a blog, too, and had been working overtime to post unflattering information about Darsey online.

Leo glanced up from his file and looked at the dog lying at his feet. The retriever lolled onto his side, exposing his belly, and his tail thumped back and forth.

"I really don't think you had anything to do with this," Leo said firmly.

Just then, his stomach growled. He sighed. *Should have stopped off at the store on the way home.* He stood up, heading toward the kitchen. "Guess it's scrambled eggs," he muttered.

The doorbell rang.

The dog jumped up and let out a friendly bark. Leo headed toward the door, peering out the peephole to see his sister sticking her tongue out at him.

Leo grinned. She was carrying something—and he hoped it was takeout. Knowing Vicki, it probably was. He opened the door and inhaled the delectable aroma of baked ziti and breadsticks. "I figured you were hungry," she said, holding up a Styrofoam container. "I brought Venezia's."

"You're the best," he said. His stomach growled.

She waved a hand as if dismissing the compliment. "I needed an excuse to come see the dog again. I fell in love when I stopped by earlier. He's the cutest thing."

As if on cue, the dog came trotting over to them.

"Have you named him?" Vicki asked, reaching down to scratch its head.

Leo sat at the kitchen table. "Um, no. Not my dog, remember? We're going to try to find its owner. If forensics does confirm that it killed Darsey, its owners are going to have to face repercussions for what happened. Not that I think he killed anyone, mind you."

The dog sat started sniffing around Vicki. She smiled and pulled a brown paper bag out of her purse. "Someone smells treats! With so much interest in my online store, I'm working on expanding my product line. Thought I'd give dog treats a try—especially now that I have such a cute test subject."

"Not duck treats?" he teased.

She made a face. "I'm afraid the market for duck treats isn't quite as big."

Leo watched in amazement as the dog scarfed down three of the honey treats. "You actually got him to eat! He hasn't eaten a thing since I brought him home."

"I'm not surprised," Vicki said. "Sounds like he went through something pretty traumatic. That really affects appetite."

Leo grabbed the pain meds off the counter. "Do you think you could get him to take one of these?"

She grinned. "I'm sure I can." She pulled out another honey treat and pressed one of the pain pills inside it, then offered it to the dog. The retriever practically inhaled it.

"So, you find anything today on the case?" Vicki asked.

He shot her a suspicious look and grabbed a breadstick. "A little. Don't even think of getting involved in this one."

She laughed aloud. "I promise I'm thinking of no such thing. I've gotten crime-solving out of my system, and I don't have any extra time right now. I'm much too busy planning your next date with Mona. I think I'll make it a double date with James and me, in fact. So, no, I'm not going to horn in on your case. Just thought I'd help you talk through it."

Nodding, he said, "Not sure if I've found anything significant. Darsey just went through a nasty divorce, and he's had some problems with protestors. Oh, and this . . ." He pulled out some paperwork he'd printed out at the station. "Turns out that Darsey Manufacturing, which was Jonathan's new brand, bought a property to build the factory on. But the property had another bidder—, from the looks of it. It's a stretch, but it could be something."

"Well," Vicki said. "That's quite a suspect list. Seems like a great start."

"Not really suspects," Leo said. "Just ideas, at this point. We're not even sure the guy was murdered. I won't be able to launch a full homicide investigation if all the evidence points to a mauling."

"Seems like they should let you follow up on the case no matter what the autopsy says. It's super weird that he was in the middle of the woods in a suit."

Leo nodded, his mouth full of doughy garlic bread.

The dog let out a whine and nudged Vicki's hand.

"He wants another treat," she squealed, pulling one more out of the bag.

"He sure does seem to like them," Leo said. "How many of those did you make?"

"Oh, I have a whole box of them in my car," Vicki said. "If he'll eat them, I'll bring them in for you. I hate to hear that he hasn't been eating."

"Hey, he's eating now. Your honey treats might have been just what he needed to perk up."

The dog wagged his tail and trotted over to Leo. He leapt up, putting both paws on Leo's lap.

"Aww, he likes you!" Vicki grinned.

"Or he's decided Italian food smells good," Leo said. "You've got a whole bowl of kibble over there, buddy."

The dog laid his head in Leo's lap, his tail wagging a hundred miles an hour.

"Yup, you have a new pet," Vicki said. "No doubt."

"I have no intention of keeping this dog. I work too much. Weird hours. It wouldn't be fair to the dog. Like I said, we'll look for its owner, and if there's no owner, we'll find it a good home."

"You know I'd totally help you out."

"Oh, yeah? I need to take you up on that," he said. "Mind coming by again tomorrow during the day to let him out?"

"No problem!" she exclaimed. "He really is a sweet dog, Leo. I can't believe you wouldn't want to keep him."

He shrugged. "I don't want to get too attached. Last thing I want is to start liking the dog and then find out he killed Darsey. They'll put him down."

But, deep down, he knew he was already getting attached. *This whole thing is trouble.*

CHAPTER 8

The following morning, Leo rolled into something wet and squishy.

What on earth . . .

He slowly blinked his eyes open. Why was a wet towel on the bed? He'd dropped his towel on the bathroom floor . . .

Oh.

He sat up.

The dog was lying at Leo's feet, legs sprawled in all directions, tongue lolling out. And the bed was *covered* in miscellaneous items from the bathroom. The rug. The plunger. The unrolled contents of an entire roll of toilet paper. His *toothbrush*.

"Seriously?" he snapped, exasperated. He snatched the toilet bowl scrubber off the spare pillow. "Why are you like this?"

Rubbing his eyes, he put everything back in the bathroom—except his toothbrush and the toilet paper, which he threw away—and nudged the dog off the bed so he could toss his sheets in the wash.

The kibble still sat untouched, so Leo broke up several of the honey-flavored treats Vicki had brought over and mixed them into the bowl. Then he added a pain pill and set the bowl back down on the ground.

"You can't just eat the treats," Leo said. "But I mixed them in with the dog food for you. Maybe that'll make the kibble more appetizing."

After sniffing around the bowl, the dog proceeded to eat happily.

"Good boy!"

Rather than heading straight to the station that morning, Leo stopped off at the county morgue. His friend Denise, the medical examiner, was ready to discuss the forensics. He was eager to find out what she'd learned.

When he arrived, the front door was unlocked, so he let himself in. Denise was pouring herself a cup of coffee in the lobby, grumbling to herself.

"Morning," he said.

She spun around with an annoyed look on her face. "Oh, good, it's you." She rolled her eyes. "You could have warned me about your new partner."

Leo cringed. "Oh yeah, Larry's back. Took me by surprise too. I was even more surprised when the chief stuck me with him on this case."

"Well, he was here this morning when I arrived," she said. "He was all demanding, prancing around my morgue like he owned the place. I wanted to sock him, but I restrained myself and only told him to shove it."

"Geez, Denise, I'm sorry," Leo said, though he couldn't help a smirk.

So, Denise put Larry in his place. Good for her.

"I mean, I've worked a few of his cases before, and he's always had a big head. But, dang, it's gotten so much worse. His stint in Boston was *not* good for him."

"At least you're not stuck with him as a partner," Leo said. "Chief put him on the Darscy case with me because he thinks it'll be a good PR move."

"Well, you got the stank end of the stick," Denise said. "Coffee?"

"Please."

She grabbed a paper cup and poured him a serving from the ancient drip coffee maker. "Well, unfortunately, my report left with him."

"Seriously?" He accepted the cup.

"Yeah. He said it was *imperative that he have it to look over.*"

He snorted out loud at her spot-on imitation of Larry's mannerisms. "We might wind up killing each other by the end of this thing," he said. "Can you do some memory recall for me?"

"I can tell you what you probably already know," she said. "Cause of death was definitely the bite to the jugular. It was canine. Found a tooth in his neck, too, so the dog bit him hard."

"A tooth?"

"Yeah. One of the incisors. So, your killer dog is missing one of its front teeth."

Missing one of its front teeth!

A big smile appeared on Leo's face, and his shoulders relaxed. "That means the dog at my house isn't our killer. Can you tell me anything else?"

"Victim had a stab wound," she said. "It wasn't the cause of death, but someone stabbed him pretty good in the leg."

That doesn't sound like your ordinary, run-of-the-mill mauling. "So, there was someone else out there with him." He took a sip of coffee. "Other than the dog."

"Two dogs, apparently. And your killer dog is still on the loose."

"That's not good. Any idea what breed?"

With a shrug, she said, "I've got a vet looking at the tooth. I don't know how much information she'll be able to give me, but she should at least be able to estimate the size of the dog, I'd think. I can also tell you that Jonathan had been dead a couple days when you found him. If I had to guess, I'd say he died Monday afternoon."

"You're the best."

"That's why I'm the boss," Denise said with a grin. "From now on, tell your partner that you can handle talking to the medical examiner, all right? I really don't think there's enough coffee in the world for me to deal with him."

"Will do," Leo said, chuckling on his way out the door. Almost as soon as he stepped out of the building, his phone rang. He cringed when Larry's name popped up on the screen. He sighed heavily, but answered. "This is Leo."

"Hey, partner! Listen, man, I got the file from the morgue. Let's meet up for lunch and talk about this case."

Leo blinked a couple times. "It's ten."

"I can eat," Larry said.

"Fine," Leo said. They decided on a nearby diner, and soon he was sitting across from Larry at a window seat, trying hard not to let his distaste show.

"So, looks like your dog probably killed Darsey. Seems pretty cut-and-dried to me." He waved the server over. "Hey, hon, refill on my coffee."

Leo blinked at Larry, then waved at the waitress. "A coffee for me, too, ma'am." Then he pulled a picture of the tooth out of the file. "Pretty sure I'd have noticed if the dog was missing a front tooth. I'll double-check, but the dog we're looking for bit Darsey hard enough to leave quite a bit of evidence behind."

Larry seemed to consider this. "Thoughts on the knife wound?"

Leo picked up the photo of Darsey's leg wound. "Looks just like the knife wound on the dog's leg."

"Hmmm . . . so someone stabbed Darsey and stabbed the dog, and then another dog bit Darsey in the throat?" Larry asked.

"Looks that way."

Larry shook his head and laughed. "Bizarre, isn't it? I sure would like to know what led up to *that* strange series of events."

"Definitely bizarre," Leo said, thinking.

"You've gotten attached to that dog, huh? You seem relieved to find out it didn't bite Darsey."

"Yeah. I mean, I wouldn't say I'm attached to it. It put a toilet brush in my bed in the middle of the night."

"That's nasty, man," Larry said, snorting.

"But I'm glad he didn't kill anyone. Wouldn't want to see him put down."

The server arrived at their table to refill the coffee, and they ordered some lunch.

"Well, I guess we could start by finding out who stabbed Darsey," Larry said.

Leo frowned. "I believe that's the point, isn't it? To find out who stabbed Darsey?"

"Well, yeah," Larry said. "We'll find out who stabbed him, and they'll be able to lead us to the real culprit."

"Real culprit?"

"The dog that bit him," Larry said.

Leo resisted the temptation to roll his eyes. "I'm less concerned about finding the dog and more concerned with finding answers. Like, why was Darsey out in the middle of the woods? Why was he stabbed, and by who? Was this just an accident, or did someone sic their dog on him?"

"You think someone might have sicced a dog on him?"

"Well, he did have a stab wound." His phone rang. "Hold on a second. It's Denise."

"She's almost as hot as Mona. No wonder you never left this town," Larry said with a wink.

Geez, he can be so creepy. Leo cringed as he answered the phone. "Hey, Denise, what ya got for me?"

"I just heard back from my vet friend," Denise said. "She thinks the tooth belongs to a retriever."

Leo frowned. "That's weird. The dog at my house is a golden retriever."

"You sure your dog isn't missing a tooth?" Denise asked.

"I'm sure," Leo said. "So, there were two retrievers at the crime scene?"

"Looks that way," Denise said.

"All right, thanks." He hung up the phone and shook his head. *Curiouser and curiouser.*

"So, your dog did kill Darsey?" Larry asked.

"One, not my dog. Two, how the heck did you get *that* out of my half of the conversation?" Leo threw up his hands, exasperated. "No, Larry, the dog at my house did not kill Darsey. But a dog of the same or similar breed did."

"Interesting," Larry said slowly. "Okay . . . so we know that there were two dogs at the crime scene, plus someone wielding a knife. But we don't know who the dogs belong to or why someone would want to stab Darsey and his dog."

"Well, I have a few leads we could follow," Leo said.

"Oh?" Larry raised an eyebrow.

"Darsey had some enemies. A bitter ex-wife and the local Go Green chapter. Also, potentially someone he outbid for the property for that new factory."

"I say we start with the ex," Larry said. "Weed that out if we can."

Leo nodded, surprised that he agreed. The server came scurrying over with their lunches. His stomach growled. He'd forgotten to eat breakfast, and his sandwich smelled delicious.

The two detectives scarfed down their lunches before heading out.

"The ex's name is Sharon Darsey," said Leo as they reached the patrol car. "She lives halfway between Magnolia Falls and Pigeon Hollow—kind of near where we found the body, actually." He made a mental note of that. Could that be relevant? "She got the estate in the divorce."

Larry shot a grin at Leo. "Let's go."

CHAPTER 9

"Whoa, would you look at that!" Larry exclaimed from the passenger seat as they pulled up to the gate to the Darsey house.

"Nice place," Leo said, eyeing the enormous black gate. A wrought iron fence wrapped around acres of fields leading up to the mansion.

"Darsey did pretty well for himself to live in a place like that," Larry said.

"His ex-wife did better," Leo murmured. They buzzed in at the gate, and a woman's voice answered over the speaker.

"May I help you?" she asked, sounding a bit annoyed.

"Hello, I'm Detective Lawson. We're looking for a Ms. Sharon Darsey."

"It's Sharon Jones now," she said. "What do you want?"

"We want to speak to you about your ex-husband."

She sighed, and the speaker clicked off. Leo glanced at Larry. Was she blowing them off? But then the gate began to creak open.

"We've obtained passage," Larry quipped.

They headed up the long driveway, pulling in front of the large home. Leo took a moment to stare up at the mansion as they climbed out of the car. He hadn't known there was a house like this anywhere in the county.

The front door opened, and a woman in a casual housedress stepped out, her arms crossed. She was about forty-five and very pretty, with an air of exhaustion about her. "Would you two like to come in?" she asked, her brow furrowed.

"Ms. Jones?" Leo asked.

"Yes."

Leo and Larry glanced at each other, and after shrugging their shoulders, they followed her inside. She led them to a formal dining room and gestured for them to take a seat across the table. For the first time, Leo saw that she had a black eye.

"Ma'am, are you all right?" Leo asked.

"I'm quite all right," she said. "I was just in the middle of a bath when you two rang in."

"Sorry to interrupt you," Larry said. "Have you been informed of what happened to Jonathan?"

She sighed, and the lines around her eyes deepened. "It was in the paper. Not exactly how I would have liked to have found out. It was quite shocking. Jonathan and I didn't exactly . . . split on the best of terms, but that sounds like an awful way to die."

"Your eye," Leo said. "When I asked if you were all right, I was asking about your bruise."

She huffed. "A parting gift from Jonathan."

"Seriously?" Larry questioned.

"Yes," she said, her voice clipped. "His occasionally abusive behavior was one of the main reasons behind the divorce, and it was also why I was a bit . . . aggressive in obtaining my divorce settlement."

"I don't recall reading anything about abuse in the court documents," Leo said.

"That was mostly discussed behind closed doors," she said. "In mediation. He didn't want his behavior going public, so I weaseled a good bit out of him."

"Why am I not buying this?" Larry asked.

Leo's jaw dropped, and he nudged Larry sharply.

But Larry just shrugged his shoulders. "I mean, why not make it public? Let the town know what an abusive creep he was?"

"Are you accusing me of lying?" she asked imperiously, but there was a haunted look in her eyes.

He seemed to realize he'd pushed too far. "Oh, no, no. Not that. I just don't feel like you're telling us everything."

Her jaw tightened, and she looked like she was about to throw them out of the house, so Leo intervened.

"Larry, that's enough," he snapped. "I'm very sorry, ma'am. Please forgive my partner. He doesn't always realize how he comes across."

Larry huffed at him.

Sharon waved her hand in their direction. "If you say so. Look, I don't know what happened. Jonathan and I haven't had anything to do with each other since the divorce. I've seen him once in the last six months—a few days ago, when he came by to talk about something. He started yelling and gave me this lovely black eye, and I threw him out and told him I wouldn't buzz him in ever again."

"I'm very sorry," Leo said.

"Might I ask you something?" Sharon leaned forward and propped her elbows on the table.

"Of course."

"The dog the paper mentioned—is it going to be put down?" she asked.

"No," Leo said. "The medical examiner confirmed that the dog found with Darsey wasn't the dog that bit him, as odd as that sounds."

"Thank goodness!" she exclaimed, jumping up out of her seat. "Give me a moment." She left the room, returning a minute later with a stack of fliers. "The paper said that the dog was a golden retriever. I about lost my mind!" She placed the fliers down. They featured a familiar golden retriever and read *Lost Dog*.

"Is that the same dog?" Larry asked Leo.

Leo stared at the photo. "That's him, all right," he said. "Ma'am, is this your dog?"

"Chippy!" Sharon said, sounding very worried. "Jonathan and I got him together a few years ago. Such a sweet dog. He would always bring Jonathan his slippers. I got him in the divorce, but he went missing recently. I was going to go out yesterday to put up these fliers, but then I read that article in the paper about Jonathan . . . I thought maybe he'd stolen the dog, and somehow Chippy had turned on him. But the idea seemed so absurd. I couldn't imagine Chippy hurting anyone, and he loved Jonathan."

Larry nodded. "This might explain why Jonathan was walking the dog so far away from town. Didn't want anyone to spot him with the dog he'd stolen."

In a suit? "You're telling me Chippy went missing a few days ago?" Leo asked.

"Yes," Sharon said. "Early Tuesday morning."

He thought back to Denise's assessment that Jonathan had been dead since Monday. *Odd.*

Sharon continued, "He's run off before, but he normally comes back by the afternoon. He's well trained. I started getting very worried yesterday, so I printed out these fliers. Then I saw that article... I was so worried that Chippy had turned on Jonathan for some reason, but that just didn't sound like Chippy. He loved Jonathan. Chippy was Jonathan's best friend. I couldn't imagine that dog hurting him."

"Is Chippy your only dog?" Leo asked.

"Yes," she said. "He was plenty of company. Always bringing us stuff from throughout the house. So silly. We've never had any other dogs."

"You didn't get any other dogs after the divorce?" Leo asked.

"No."

"How about Jonathan?" Larry asked.

"Not that I know of," she said. "Jonathan was pretty torn up about me getting Chippy. That's why he hit me—because I wouldn't give him Chippy."

"I'm assuming you want your dog back?" Larry asked.

Leo frowned. Truthfully, despite his best efforts, he *had* gotten a little too attached to the dog. But it was fine. Or, at least, it would be fine. He'd known they would have to look for the owner. It was better for Chippy to go back to his person.

Besides, Leo didn't exactly enjoy waking up next to a toilet brush.

Sharon smiled. "Oh, definitely! I'm so glad the police found him. He's okay, isn't he?"

"He's fine," Leo said. "He's actually been staying with me. You're welcome to come get him anytime."

"Thank you!" she said, clapping a hand over her heart. "Call me when you get off work, and I'll come by and get him. I'm so glad he's okay."

"Of course," Leo said, writing down her phone number.

They asked her a few more questions about Jonathan, and Leo felt good about her answers. If he had to bet, he'd say she was telling the truth. When they finished, he shook her hand.

"See you later this afternoon," he said as he and Larry headed out.

She closed the door behind them, and Leo exhaled heavily at the thought of giving up the dog. Mona, he imagined, would be disappointed, as would Vicki.

"I don't know about that," Larry grumbled as they walked toward the patrol car.

"About what?" Leo asked.

"About her. I don't know if what she was selling was right."

"Meaning . . ."

"I don't believe Darsey gave her that black eye. She was kind of flinchy when she was talking about it."

"I imagine it was traumatic to relive," Leo said stiffly.

"Maybe," Larry said. "She was hiding *something*, I'm pretty sure. But, hey, I could be wrong. I bet you're relieved."

"How so?" Leo asked, opening the car door.

"That you're able to get rid of that dog now," he said. "I sure would be. I'd be ticked if I got stuck babysitting some dog from a crime scene. They should have taken that thing straight to the pound if they thought he might have hurt Darsey."

"But he didn't," Leo reminded him.

Larry grunted. "Want to go check out that Go Green group? They've got some sort of meet-and-greet thing going on today downtown. Getting signatures for something."

"How'd you hear about that?" Leo asked.

"They posted fliers. Sounds like there's going to be a bunch of them there, including their little ringleader."

"What are they trying to get signatures for?"

"I think to try to stop the factory from being built," Larry said. "Although, with Darsey gone, who knows if that's even going to happen now."

"This Go Green chapter, from what I've read online, is pretty large. That gives us a number of suspects to sift through," Leo said. "But we can start with the leaders. Get a feel for them and see if any of them raise a red flag."

"Agreed," Larry said, buckling his seat belt and changing the radio station to the most obnoxious, twangy country-blues mess that could be found. "Let's get going."

CHAPTER 10

"This doesn't look like a bunch of tree huggers protesting," Larry said as they parked the patrol car down the street from what looked to be some grand celebration.

"I think you're right about that," Leo said.

There were guitarists set up on a small stage, vendors passing out green-themed merchandise, and smiling people in Go Green T-shirts.

"You don't think they're celebrating what happened to Darsey, do you?" asked Leo.

"That's messed up," Larry said as they piled out of the car.

They made their way into the crowded downtown, taking time to let the scenery sink in. Everyone seemed incredibly excited about something—and not just about the cotton candy vendor. But Leo wasn't quite sure what.

A young man stepped out on stage when the guitarists paused between songs. He was wearing one of the Go Green T-shirts and a matching ball cap.

Leo nudged Larry, nodding toward the stage.

"Who's that?" Larry asked.

"Kirk Walter," Leo whispered. "The leader of the Go Green chapter. I recognize him from my preliminary research."

They watched as Kirk grabbed the microphone, and all eyes went to him. Several people wearing the Go Green shirts began clapping, then the rest of the crowd joined in.

"Thank you for that warm welcome, everyone," Kirk said, grinning ear to ear. "Today *was* going to be a protest, but instead we're celebrating a Go Green victory! The Darsey family informed us just yesterday that they will *not* be continuing with their plans of building the boot factory here in our town!"

Uproarious applause broke out.

Kirk waited for the crowd to calm down, then continued, "That factory would have had devastating effects on our local environment —especially on the river where, undoubtedly, the waste would have been dumped. Thanks to all of our efforts and collaboration in the past twenty-four hours, I am happy to say that our future generations will be able to enjoy clean air and clean, local water."

More clapping, although Kirk calmed the crowd more quickly this time around. "Now, for those of you who don't know, this is a rather bittersweet victory. Jonathan Darsey, the gentleman who was bringing this atrocity to town, was attacked by a dog and killed. While Mr. Darsey and Go Green have had their spats in the past, I want to make sure we are perfectly clear about what we are celebrating here today. We are not celebrating the tragic end of a businessman—just the fact that our town won't be polluted. I want to take a moment to thank his relatives for agreeing to put a stop to the factory. And I especially want to report that we've gotten word about what will be going down on the Darsey Manufacturing land now. The family has informed me that they are selling the property to another bidder who had an interest in it. Our town will soon be home to a roller rink!"

People clapped excitedly, especially the children and their parents.

"That's cool," Larry said. "Can't say I disagree with the crowd here. I'd rather have a roller rink than a factory emitting a bunch of smog all day long."

"Yeah, it's definitely the better option." Still, the scene left Leo with an unsettled feeling in the pit of his stomach. "That factory would have brought a bunch of jobs to the area, though."

"The roller rink will, too, though probably not as many."

Kirk continued speaking into the microphone, and it looked like he was going to be up there for another few minutes.

Leo nudged Larry and whispered, "Why don't we split up on this one? Try to talk to as many of the Go Green folks as possible."

"Should be easy, since they're all wearing neon-green T-shirts," Larry said. "All right. Let's see what we can find out."

Leo was glad to not have Larry with him while he went around talking with various Go Greeners. He approached a girl with pink hair. "Detective Leo Lawson," he said. "Could I ask you a few questions?"

She snapped her gum and looked bored. "Sure."

"How long have you been involved in this Go Green chapter?" he asked.

"Mmm, about a year." She cracked her neck from side to side.

"Oh, great! Had you ever met Jonathan Darsey personally?"

She shook her head. "No, but Kirk wrote a lot about him on the blog. Seemed like a real jerk. Did you know he beat his wife? They're divorced now. Good for her."

After a few more questions, Leo realized she didn't know anything more than the internet gossip he'd already read, and he moved on to a muscled guy with bleach-blond hair and a jacket with a surfboard on it.

After Leo introduced himself, he asked, "How long have you been involved in this Go Green chapter?"

The wannabe surfer squinted and shrugged. "I dunno, dude. Six months or a year?"

"What got you involved?"

He shot a conspiratorial grin at Leo. "Dude. There's this cute girl who's really into it. I'm trying to impress her."

Leo suppressed an eyeroll. "Did you know Jonathan Darsey personally?"

"Who?"

Leo stared at him. "Jonathan Darsey? The businessman who was attacked by the dog?"

Wannabe Surfer looked confused.

"He was going to build that factory?"

Recognition appeared on Wannabe Surfer's face. "Oh, yeah. Him . . . Wait, what about him?"

Leo thought he might scream. He'd finally found someone who rivaled Larry in intelligence. "Had you ever met him?"

"Nah, dude. I went to a protest on that land he bought, but that's it."

"Do you know anyone here who might have interacted with him more?"

He shrugged. "Nah, dude. Sorry."

Leo thanked him for his time and moved on. The next woman he talked to was about twenty-two, with a dark pixie cut.

"Did you know Jonathan Darsey personally?" Leo asked.

"Oh, not at all," she said. "I've read Kirk's blogs, of course."

"Do you know anyone here who might have interacted with him more?"

She shook her head slowly. "I think you're barking up the wrong tree, pal. It's not personal. None of this is personal. We're not the kind of tree huggers who throw paint on old ladies wearing fur coats. We protested the land, and we tried to stir up community opposition to the factory, but I don't think anyone would have confronted Darsey in person. Besides"—her nose wrinkled—"wasn't he killed by a dog? What are you even doing here?"

"He *was* killed by a dog," said Leo, maintaining a neutral expression. "We're just required to cross all our t's and dot all our i's before we wrap up the case."

Two more interviews got him similar answers.

Through the crowd, he spotted Larry chowing down on some cotton candy. Half of the blue spun sugar fell off the stick and dropped to the ground. Larry stared at the lost treat as if he were five, his jaw agape. Leo suppressed a laugh.

Why was Larry even here in Magnolia Falls? The man had a degree from Harvard; what was he doing working as a small-town cop? Shouldn't he be at the FBI or something? Leo felt in his gut that there was something Larry wasn't telling him. He'd do a little side investigation into Larry later. There had to be a real reason he was back in town. Leo was pretty sure it wasn't really about family drama. He knew Larry's parents—everyone in town did. They seemed perfectly healthy and stable.

Oh, how he hoped that Boston PD had cut Larry loose for incompetence.

Leo pushed the thoughts aside for the time being. He still had several Go Greeners to interview. He continued working his way through the crowd, remaining friendly and personable to encourage the protestors to talk to him. Most were as helpful as they could be, but it seemed like they just didn't have information. Could he find Kirk Walter and talk to him? He looked around. The man seemed to have disappeared after his little speech onstage.

He started asking if anyone had seen Kirk. Eventually, someone said he'd gone out to the parking lot to get more Go Green merchandise, as the booth was running low. Leo headed toward the parking lot and spotted a white van with a giant Go Green logo on the side.

And then he spotted Larry—already talking to Kirk.

He had to give it to the man, he had decent instincts. He'd beat Leo to the morgue *and* to questioning the Go Green leader. Leo hurried toward them.

"Are you kidding me? You must be joking!" Kirk roared, pointing an accusing finger in Larry's direction.

Larry wore a smug look. "I asked a simple question."

"No, you really didn't!" Kirk shouted. "Get out of my face. I know my rights!"

Leo raced over. "Whoa, whoa, whoa. What's going on here, Larry?"

"I'll tell you what's going on!" Kirk shouted and jerked his thumb toward Larry. "Your buddy here just accused me of killing Jonathan Darsey!"

Leo instinctively smacked his own forehead, shaking his head. "Larry, are you serious right now?"

"Yeah, I am!" Larry exclaimed, then held up a long knife. "Look what I found on him!"

Leo paused and took the knife from Larry, studying it for a moment. "Mr. Walter, are you aware that this state has a legal limit on the length of a switchblade?"

Kirk's face turned bright red. "Um . . . well . . . honestly, no . . . I'm from Minnesota."

"You brought this knife with you from Minnesota? I'm assuming you didn't fly," Leo replied.

"No, my mom and I moved here a couple years ago. The knife was my late father's. It was in a box on a moving van. I . . . didn't know it was illegal."

Leo handed the knife back to Kirk. "If it's a family heirloom, you can get special licensing to hold onto it, but you definitely can't be using it out and about. It will need to remain in a case of some sort at home. Now, that being said . . ." Leo turned to Larry. "Why are you accusing him of hurting Darsey just because he's got a knife on him?"

"Did you not see that knife? It's a fit for—"

"It *definitely* isn't," Leo said before Larry could finish his sentence. "Did you even look at the photos in the case file? That thin blade wouldn't have done the type of damage inflicted on Darsey."

"Wait, wait, wait," Kirk said. "Wasn't Darsey attacked by a dog?"

"He was," Leo said. "After he was stabbed."

"Whoa," Kirk said, paling. "The papers didn't say nothing about that."

"Have you been in contact with the Darsey family?" Leo asked.

"Not face-to-face. His heirs are out-of-towners—a niece and nephew in Chicago. They sent an email informing us of the decision to sell the land to the other bidder," Kirk explained. "I guess they didn't want us protesting anymore." He pulled out his phone and showed the email to Leo.

Leo took a look at it. "Interesting. Good to know. I apologize for my partner's abrasiveness, Kirk."

"Hey!" Larry nudged Leo. "The guy got snippy with me!"

"Larry, maybe you should take a walk," Leo suggested.

Larry crossed his arms and set his jaw.

With a sigh, Leo decided not to push the issue. He turned back to Kirk. "Is there anything more you could tell us about your . . . relationship with Jonathan Darsey?"

"I met with him once or twice," Kirk said. "Real arrogant fellow. Talked to me like I was a moron. From what I hear, that's how he talked to everyone. Wasn't nice to that ex-wife of his either. And he didn't care at all about what sort of impact his factory was going to have on the environment. His past record was just awful. He poisoned rivers and always did the bare minimum when it came to remaining environmentally friendly."

Leo nodded and gestured for Kirk to continue.

"His previous factories skirted worker-safety requirements too. Someone lost a foot due to negligence and a lack of safety precautions. Our town didn't need this factory. I know it would have brought jobs, but would we really want a place like that here? Working for Darsey was hazardous. I'm glad the factory's been canceled."

Kirk paused and trained a long, serious look on Leo. "But I never would have hurt the man to stop the factory from being built. The whole reason I didn't want it built was because of the damage it would have caused to people. I care about people, and I care about the environment. I didn't want to see anyone around here getting hurt—and frankly, that includes Darsey. I wanted him to do better, not die. I hate what happened to him. That's not a way I'd want anyone to go."

"Well, I appreciate your cooperation, Kirk," Leo said. "Do you mind if I take down your personal number so I can contact you if I have any follow-up questions?"

"Sure," Kirk said. "So, you're investigating this as a murder, then? Man, I really thought it was just an unfortunate accident. Sort of wish we'd just canceled the protest instead of throwing a celebration."

"At the moment, the public believes it was an accident," Leo said. "And I wouldn't say we're *necessarily* investigating a murder. But at minimum, someone left the man out there to die alone. We need to find out who was there so we can piece together exactly what happened."

"Understood," Kirk said, scribbling down his information for Leo. "And . . . um . . . I'm sorry about the knife. I've used it at events because it fits in my pocket easily, and you never know when you're going to need a knife to cut some string or open a box or whatever. I'll get it licensed and keep it at home."

"Be sure that you do," Leo said. "I'm not going to cite you for it, but I will be following up to make sure you've done your part."

"I will," Kirk said. "Thank you, Detective."

Leo nodded, and he and Larry slowly made their way away from the event, heading to Leo's patrol car. Knots were forming in his neck from the stress of working alongside Larry.

He couldn't wait for the day to be over.

CHAPTER 11

Leo's nerves were absolutely shot by the time he arrived back home that evening. The day with Larry had almost been more than he could handle. There had been multiple times, in fact, when he'd wanted to punch the man in the face.

How could someone with Larry's background be so childish and unprofessional? He had a Harvard degree and had landed a job among big-city police. But it was almost unfathomable how inappropriate he'd been all day. Did, perhaps, his behavior have something to do with why he was no longer working in Boston? Had he *really* been transferred? After spending the day with him and seeing what his work conduct was like, it wouldn't have surprised Leo if he'd come crawling back to Magnolia Falls with his tail between his legs after being fired.

As Leo parked in the driveway, he received a text from Mona: *I was hanging out with Vicki today, so we came by to feed the dog and let him out. He's so sweet, and I'm so glad you were able to save him that day. I absolutely adore him. Hope to talk to you later!*

Leo sighed. He was going to have to tell Mona he'd found the dog's owner. He decided to give her a call, and she answered, peppy as ever.

"Hey, Leo!" she sang. "I guess you got my text. You home now?"

"Yeah, just getting home. Thought I'd let you know we found the dog's owner," he said. "Jonathan Darsey's ex-wife is claiming him. Says his name's Chippy. She and Jonathan bought him together when they were married, and she got him in the divorce."

"Oh, wow!" Mona said sadly. Then her voice brightened, as if she were trying to keep up a brave face. "Well, that's great news. Is she coming to get him?"

"Not until later tonight. Thought I'd see if you wanted to come over and say bye to him."

"Definitely!" she exclaimed. "I'll be there soon!"

Leo hung up the phone before heading inside. The dog came running up to him, wagging his tail and barking excitedly as he did a little spin.

"Chippy?" Leo asked.

The dog sat upright, his ears perking up and his tail picking up speed.

Leo sighed. "Looks like we found your person. But at least you're cleared of killing Jonathan. You're safe now."

He walked toward the back of the house, opening the door into the yard. Chippy bolted outside, running a lap around the perimeter to release some of his pent-up energy.

Leo watched Chippy run for several minutes. The dog was full of life, and it was the most playful thing Leo had ever seen. Soon, Mona arrived, and the three of them found themselves hanging out in the backyard. Mona had brought a tennis ball, and Chippy proved to be quite adamant about playing fetch.

"He's such a good dog," Mona said, scratching Chippy behind the ear as he gave her the tennis ball Leo had just thrown. "I hate that you're not going to be able to keep him."

Leo frowned. Truthfully, he *had* grown attached. "It really is a shame," he admitted. "I was starting to like him. Maybe I'll consider getting myself a dog."

"Aww, you're not going to be able to find a dog like this anywhere," Mona said. "He's one of a kind."

"Definitely," Leo said. "Though hopefully whatever dog I adopt won't put the toilet brush on my pillow."

Mona laughed aloud, and they headed inside, Chippy right on

their heels. "So . . . I brought over some ingredients for a new jam recipe I'm going to try."

"You want me to help you make jam?" he asked with a smile.

"Well, our last date didn't exactly go as planned," she said. "I figured a date night doing something simple like making jam wasn't going to end in murder."

"Good point," Leo said, grinning as he followed Mona into the kitchen. "I'd love to help you make some jam."

"Excellent! Wash your hands!"

Leo walked over to an antique record player he'd inherited from his grandfather and glanced through the records. He put on George Strait, and the strains of "I Cross My Heart" filtered through the house.

He said, "This okay? The cover band was playing it at the Fall Festival, and I've been humming it ever since."

A soft smile flickered across her face. "It's perfect."

Chippy sat and watched them as they mashed up the ingredients, working hard to get everything just right. Before too long, Chippy had wandered off and they'd completed some apple butter jam. Much to Leo's delight, the apple butter and fig preserves tasted excellent.

Almost as soon as they'd sampled the jam, Chippy returned with a book in his mouth, nudging Mona's hand as if to give it to her. She laughed and accepted the present, setting it on the counter.

"Would *you* like to try some jam?" she asked. She put a little on her finger, and Chippy licked up the jam just as enthusiastically as he'd devoured Vicki's honey treats.

"You've got a sweet tooth, huh?" she cooed.

The doorbell rang, and Leo frowned.

It was time to say farewell to his dog friend.

He answered the door, and sure enough, Sharon had arrived.

"Sharon," he said, stepping aside. "Come on in."

"Thank you," she replied. She followed him to the kitchen, and Chippy sat up when he saw her.

"Look, Chippy," Mona said. "It's your mommy."

Chippy wagged his tail unenthusiastically.

Sharon smiled, but it seemed forced. "Hey, Chippy! I was wondering where you got off to, boy!"

Chippy meandered over to Sharon and rubbed up against her. She scratched him behind the ears.

Leo studied the two of them. Something wasn't right.

"Good boy," she said, pulling out a leash. "Okay, let's get you home. Thank you two so much for watching over him." She hooked the leash onto Chippy's collar and started toward the door, but Chippy dead-weighted her. "Chippy! Come on, boy!"

The dog whined and continued to lie flat on the ground.

"Oh, dear," Mona said. "Is everything all right?"

Sharon sighed, dropping the leash in frustration. "Honestly?"

"I'd prefer it that way," Leo said slowly.

"Chippy was always Jonathan's dog," she said. "Jonathan loved Chippy to death. Sometimes I was certain he loved the dog more than me. I . . . never really wanted a dog."

"Then why did you fight for Chippy during the divorce?" Leo asked, exasperated.

Sharon paused, then admitted, "Out of spite. He cheated on me and hurt me. I was so angry and bitter about the whole thing. I wanted to hurt him back, and I knew how much he cared about Chippy. Honestly, I even had my lawyer convinced that I just had to have the dog. I had the judge convinced too. I wound up walking out with Chippy."

Leo crossed his arms. "He cheated? Why didn't you mention the affair when my partner and I were at your home earlier?"

Sharon paused, her eyes widening. "Um . . . I didn't think it was relevant. Do you think it could be?"

"It certainly could be," he said. "If your ex-husband was cheating on you, that could help us find a possible motive."

Her demeanor shifted. "Yeah, a bitter ex-wife who was so angry about his affairs that she'd fight to have his dog taken away *would* make a viable suspect, am I right?" she demanded. "But I did tell you that he hit me, which seems like more than enough information to clue you in to the fact that I hated him. Loathed him. But the divorce was finalized months ago. I've had a chance to cool off. I certainly didn't want him dead."

"You were still angry," Leo said. "You could have given Chippy back to him when he came to your home recently."

"Okay, fine. I'm still angry," Sharon spat. "But . . . that's all. Just angry. There's a big gap between *angry* and wishing harm on someone. I didn't wish him harm, and I certainly wouldn't have hurt him."

A thread came back to Leo. The microchip! Chippy's owner had wiped all the information off his microchip. He studied Sharon. "Why did you call in and have all the information taken off your dog's microchip?"

She blinked. "Microchip?"

He waited for her to continue, but she seemed baffled.

"I don't know what you're talking about," she said finally. "What's a microchip?"

Leo glanced from Sharon to Mona. "You know, it's imbedded in Chippy's shoulder? It can be scanned at any vet or animal shelter so that if he's ever lost, the person who finds him can get your contact info and reunite you? But the company said all the contact information was taken off last Friday."

Her brow furrowed. "Last Friday? Jonathan . . . came to see me Friday morning. That's when he demanded Chippy and hit me when I wouldn't acquiesce."

Mona made a sympathetic noise.

"And you didn't call the microchip company?" Leo asked.

She ran a hand through her hair. "No! I wouldn't even know how to call them. I didn't even know what a microchip was, or that he has one."

Chippy was sitting on one of Leo's feet and sniffing at his hand, his tail wagging happily. Leo scratched Chippy's head, his mind turning over the new information. "Good boy," he muttered.

Sharon watched the interaction, sighing. "I don't suppose . . . *you* would want him?"

That caught Leo's attention, sending all thoughts of microchips flying from his head. "Me?"

"He clearly likes you," Sharon said. "He used to sit on Jonathan's foot like that. Curl up with him. Chippy just sort of exists in my house, you know? I can tell you like him. I'm a lazy pet owner. I don't even take Chippy for walks; heck, I hired my boyfriend's son to walk him because I can't be bothered. But he's a good dog, and he deserves an owner who actually likes dogs. I think he'd be happier with you."

He wasn't so sure about adopting a dog, but when he caught Mona's eye, he felt encouraged. She was grinning ear to ear.

"All right," he said. "Honestly, I've grown to really like him. I wouldn't mind adopting him."

"Oh, excellent!" Sharon exclaimed. She chuckled. "I imagine that's what Jonathan would have wanted. For Chippy to go to a good home, with a dog person."

"I do want a little more information about the affairs Jonathan had," Leo said. "And your phone records for Friday."

"Of course," Sharon said. "And, you're right. I should have mentioned the affairs to you when you came to speak to me earlier. Honestly, your partner was making me uncomfortable, and I was trying to get through the interview as quickly as possible."

"Larry has a tendency to do that," he said.

He ran through the evidence in his head, setting aside the question of the microchip for a second. Darsey had been attacked with a knife, which suggested either an assailant he trusted, someone his own size, or someone skilled enough to land a blow against a person bigger and stronger. There didn't seem to be a lot of trust between Jonathan and Sharon, and she didn't give the impression of being a skilled fighter. Plus, if she wasn't a dog person, how could she have sicced a dog on him to deliver the killing bite?

But he couldn't rule out her ability to fight just by looking at her. What if she had a martial arts background?

He had an idea. "Catch," he called, grabbing a pen off the table and gently tossing it toward her.

She glanced up, startled, and flailed at the pen as she tried to catch it, sending it clattering to the floor. Chippy trotted toward the pen, picked it up, and brought it back to Leo.

"What . . . was that about?" Sharon asked.

"Sorry about that," Leo said, taking the pen from Chippy and grabbing a piece of paper. "Would you mind just writing down the basic details of Jonathan's affairs? Anything you know? Names, dates, that sort of thing?"

"Oh, sure," she said. While she jotted down the information, Leo's mind raced. A trained fighter would have caught the pen, or at least made a better effort at it—not batted it down with all the grace of a confused pigeon.

And if Sharon hadn't canceled the information on the microchip, that must mean *Jonathan* had called the company. This was getting stranger and stranger.

She finished and handed Leo the paper. "Just make sure you give Chippy plenty of walks. He can get pretty antsy if you keep him locked up too much. I cannot tell you how many pairs of shoes he's chewed up."

Leo thanked Sharon, and she left, leaving him alone with Chippy and a very excited Mona.

"You have a dog!" Mona shrieked as soon as the door closed. "And he's the cutest dog ever!" She clapped her hands and got down on her knees to pet Chippy and scratch behind his ears.

"Looks that way." He plopped down on the couch.

Oh, gosh. What had he done?

CHAPTER 12

*M*ona sat next to Leo on the couch, and Chippy found a comfortable spot on the floor in front of them, wagging his tail.

"You want to stay here with me, Chippy?" Leo asked, and the dog seemed to perk up.

"I think I should get a pet of some sort," Mona said. "I mean, Vicki has her duck and her bees; now you have a dog. What do you think?"

"You seem like someone who would own a bunny."

"A bunny!" she exclaimed with a laugh. "Why a bunny?"

"I don't know. You're cute, and you seem like you would like a cute little pet like that."

She blushed. "Well . . . honestly . . . I probably would . . ." She chuckled. "Oh, my . . . I think you know me better than I know myself, because now I want to go to the pet store to get a bunny."

Leo bit back a snort. Then the day came rushing back to him, and he groaned and sank down into the couch.

"Long day?" she asked.

"The longest," he complained. "The chief stuck me with the oaf of the office for this case. And he's been causing problems ever since we started."

"Oh, I'm sorry," she murmured. "What kind of problems?"

"First, he goes ahead of me to get the autopsy report and alienates the medical examiner. He holds the report hostage until I agree to waste time having lunch with him at ten in the morning. And he accuses every single person we interview of murder! Straight-up accuses them without any evidence. It was ridiculous. He got into it with just about every single person we interacted with today."

"Yuck," Mona said. "Sounds like a real head case."

"You have no idea. This guy . . . this guy is nuts. And he thinks he's better than everyone else. Struts around the office like he owns the place, and everyone just falls for the act."

"Is he new? Maybe he just doesn't realize how he comes across."

He rolled his eyes. "He just got transferred from a big-city station, and he acts like that makes him some sort of expert. I mean, at first, I thought about listening to him. Seeing if he had some insight, given his background. But the man has no idea what he's doing! I'm starting to wonder if he was lying about his reason for transfer."

"What reason did he give?" she asked.

"That he came home to get back to his roots. That he had some family drama to sort out. Between you and me, I think he was probably let go at the other station for behavioral problems or general incompetence. His conduct is just terrible."

Mona made a sympathetic noise. "Well, I hope you give him a real chance. Maybe he'll get better in time."

Leo grumbled, but Chippy jumped up onto the couch, squishing both of them under his weight. They laughed and eventually managed to wiggle into a more comfortable position. She fell asleep with her head on Leo's chest. He caressed her hair, his heart practically bursting.

Yep, this was *definitely* a better date.

* * *

LEO RUBBED HIS TEMPLES AS HE SAT BEHIND HIS DESK ON SATURDAY. Larry had stationed himself just outside the cubicle to tell grandiose stories . . . again.

I'm going to wind up strangling him before we wrap this up, Leo thought, trying his best to concentrate on the reading he was doing for the case. Jonathan Darsey had evidently had some business troubles; it looked like Sharon had gotten all of his factories in the divorce and was now the owner of Darsey Industrial. The new property in Magnolia Falls was under Jonathan's new brand, Darsey Manufacturing.

Did that mean anything?

"So, needless to say, the punk wound up getting a two-year sentence," Larry said, finally reaching the end of the ridiculous story. "But the chief gave me a promotion after that one." His fellow officers all laughed, and Leo thunked his head down onto the desk.

Then he heard Ann butt in.

"Hey, boys, break it up, would you?" she called. "Larry, I know you're not *really* the rookie, but you know the rules 'round here. You left, so that makes you the new fella. You get to do the coffee run. Scram, would you?"

Larry laughed. "Oh, is Miss Ann giving me a hard time?" he asked in a taunting tone.

Leo poked his head out of the cubicle with a wry grin.

"She is," Ann said, slapping Larry's chest with a slip of paper. "But don't worry. I did the grunt work for you and took everyone's orders, *rookie*."

"I ain't no rookie!" Larry exclaimed, and the other men standing around all burst into raucous laughter.

"She got you, Larry!"

"Oh, listen to Ann, man, she'll bite your head off!"

"Get the woman her coffee, Larry!"

"Get mine with an extra shot of expresso!"

Larry huffed and snatched the slip of paper. In an attempt to save face, he performed a dramatic bow. "Whatever the pretty lady wishes, I suppose. I'll go get everyone some blasted coffee. You're all a bunch of spoiled small-town cops . . . In the big city, we don't have time for coffee runs. We drink our coffee from the break room, if we're lucky."

"Just go get the coffee, Larry," Ann drawled.

Larry headed out the door, and the Saturday shift officers—who were evidently part of the Larry Simmons Fan Club—dispersed.

Ann leaned against the wall of Leo's cubicle. "I got you a few minutes of solace."

"You're wonderful," he said, grinning and rolling his chair back to the desk. "He's driving me insane."

"I can tell. He's obnoxious, and I can't believe how googly-eyed everyone around here has gotten over him. Anyway, I'm off. Solved those burglaries, so now I'm stuck doing traffic duty in front of the schools."

"They still got you doing bullcrap like that?" he asked. "When you just solved a case in record time?"

"You know how it works around here." She rolled her eyes. "If a *lady*"—she imitated Larry's intonation on the word *lady*—"wants to be taken seriously as a cop, she can't be average. She's got to be the best."

"Sorry, Ann," he said with a wince. "But, let's be honest, you're better than most of these baboons."

"Oh, I know that," she said with a wink. "But *better* isn't the same as the *best*. And until I'm the best—maybe second best—I'll never be treated as average."

She headed out the door, and Leo shook his head. Ann deserved to be doing more than directing traffic in the mornings. She might be best or second best in the department already. She was certainly a better cop than he would ever be, he felt—*definitely* better than Larry Simpleton Simmons.

Leo went back to work on his computer, looking up the women that Jonathan had supposedly cheated with. He also began looking into the piece of property that Jonathan had intended to build his factory on. After about half an hour of research, he found the name of the person who was now purchasing the property. And, much to Leo's surprise, he immediately recognized the name: Sheldon Goldberg.

"What?" Leo yelped.

Sheldon was friends with Mona's Aunt Bee, as a long-time member of Aunt Bee's Coupon Clippers. Leo had met him on a number of occasions, and the man seemed as harmless as a newborn bunny. Was it even possible that Sheldon could be involved in something like this?

Leo doubted it. He pulled out his phone, texting Mona to ask if she knew anything about Sheldon purchasing land.

She messaged back at once. *Hey, I'm close and have something for you. Why don't I swing by and we can chat? ;)*

He smiled approvingly and texted, *Sounds great!*

Five minutes later, she entered his cubicle carrying a to-go mug, which she placed on his desk. "I brought you some more tea with Vicki's honey spoons. She said you really liked them, and she brought some into the store."

"I appreciate it," he said, grinning. Mona was so thoughtful.

"So, what about Sheldon?" she asked.

"Turns out Sheldon is buying that property that Darsey was going to build his factory on. I'm a little worried."

"About Sheldon? You really think he could be involved?" Mona asked, her nose wrinkling.

"Unfortunately, I can't let my personal relationship with Sheldon interfere with my investigation. I need to go talk to him."

"Well," Mona said, thinking for a moment. "There's a Coupon Clippers meeting at the library in an hour. I was going to skip it, but I could go and bring you with me. Sheldon's always there. He's the club secretary."

"You are wonderful." He jumped up. "Let's get out of here before my temporary partner gets back."

"That bad, huh?"

"The worst."

"Maybe you just need to give him time."

But it was too late to avoid Larry. The oaf of the office came marching into the station, shouting, "I have arrived, fellas! Got your coffee! Come get it while it's hot!" He set the coffees down and then spotted Mona. His eyes lit up, and he made a beeline toward the two of them.

Leo groaned aloud, and Mona's face remained neutral.

"Oh, you didn't tell me your partner was Larry Simmons," she said.

Leo sighed. "That's the one."

"Mona!" Larry called. "My goodness, beautiful as ever, I see. Heard you were opening the shop soon? I'm impressed."

"Thanks, Larry," she said with a pasted-on smile. "I was just leaving, actually."

"Aww, you can't come strutting up here looking so gorgeous and not stick around to play catch-up with me."

"I really do have to go," she said, then offered Leo a real smile. "I just remembered I have to let a contractor into the store. I'll see you soon."

"See you later, Mona."

She hurried out of the station, and Leo hoped her rush was a bid to avoid Larry.

"You look like you're getting ready to leave," Larry said. "Where are we heading, partner?"

Leo sighed. Was there any way to ditch him? He couldn't come up with a good excuse. "To the library. The Coupon Clippers are having a meeting, and one of their members is a friend of mine who might have some information."

"Excellent!" Larry said, picking up one of the coffees for himself. "Let's roll, partner!"

Leo sent Mona a warning text: *Larry coming to Coupon Clippers. Sorry.*

A moment later, she replied, *I'm so sorry, but is it okay if I don't come?*

Snorting, he typed, *I don't blame you a bit. I wouldn't want to see more of him either.*

She replied, *Oh, it's not that. I really should be here while the electrician is fixing the lights in the back of the shop. He didn't do it right the first time, and we're getting way too close to opening day.*

Honestly, he was disappointed that she wasn't trying to avoid Larry.

As soon as the two of them loaded up into Leo's patrol car, Larry started heckling Leo. "You know, Mona and I went out the summer after she and I graduated high school."

Leo cringed. "Really?"

He hadn't interacted with Larry much back then. Larry was two years younger and had gone to a fancy private school, while Leo, Vicki, and Mona had all been in the local public school district. He *definitely* hadn't realized Larry and Mona had actually dated. Was that why she'd been so carefully neutral in the interaction back at the station?

"Oh, yeah. Didn't work out—what with me heading off to Harvard and all. She's a babe. You're a lucky man."

"Yes, I am." Leo's stomach churned uncomfortably at the thought that Larry actually dated Mona. Should he ask Mona if it was true or if Larry was just blowing smoke? How would she take a question like that? Did it even matter?

"Man, she is so hot," Larry said.

Leo had to resist reaching over to the passenger's seat to punch the man.

"I'm telling you. You don't find women like that anymore. That natural sexy look, you know?"

"Please stop," Leo snapped. "I'd rather focus on our case, all right?"

"Oh, my bad, man. I imagine thinking about Mona gets you pretty distracted, am I right?"

Leo let out a sigh of relief when they finally arrived at the library. The drive only took five minutes, but it felt like five years. "Hey, listen," Leo said as they walked through the automatic doors. "This guy and I have a history. I think we should split duties a little bit today."

"Ooh, wanna do the whole good-cop, bad-cop bit?"

You're joking. Leo suppressed an eyeroll. Barely. "No, man, I don't want to do that. Listen—you brought your work laptop. I want you to go look into these names." Leo handed Larry a slip of paper. "Sharon gave me a list of women she believes Jonathan cheated on her with. You look into them, and I'll go talk to this guy."

"Sounds like a plan," Larry said, trotting off with the list in hand.

Thank goodness. Leo headed toward the meeting rooms. When he found the right one, he paused in the doorway. Aunt Bee was standing in front, heading up the meeting. And much to his surprise, it looked like Aunt Cee, Aunt Bee's sister, was back in town. The woman liked to talk about her lavish vacations and affairs with younger men, both of which drove Aunt Bee insane.

"Would you hush?" Aunt Bee snapped at Aunt Cee.

"Me? You're the one boring everyone," Aunt Cee replied, studying her manicured fingernails.

"Why do you come to my Coupon Clippers meetings if you're not going to participate?" Aunt Bee retorted.

Leo chuckled and waved Sheldon down. The man nodded in his direction and stood up.

"Those two at it again?" Leo asked quietly when Sheldon reached him.

Sheldon laughed. "Aunt Bee and Aunt Cee? Always."

"Mind if we step out for a second?" Leo asked. "I need to talk to you."

"Of course," Sheldon said.

Sheldon was a middle-aged gentleman, and the only man in Coupon Clippers. He'd recently started dating a group member named Alana—a single mom with a wildly successful blog.

"Always good to see you, Leo. What can I do for you?" Sheldon asked when they reached the sliding doors that led out to the sidewalk.

"I want to ask you about that property you're buying," Leo said. "For a roller rink, I've heard?"

"Isn't it something?" Sheldon said excitedly. "I mean, I know I shouldn't be too happy. It's a real shame what happened to Jonathan Darsey. I didn't know the man personally, but I heard a dog got him. Can't imagine! I've just recently decided to open the roller rink—I sent in a bid on that property on impulse, to tell you the truth—but the more I've learned about the land the last couple days, the more excited I've gotten. It's a perfect tract for a rink and will allow me room to expand the business over time."

"Why a roller rink?" Leo asked.

Sheldon shifted. "I know it sounds silly, but it's been a dream of mine. And it's a solid business idea—we don't have enough activities for kids in this town, and there isn't a roller rink within fifty miles. I was worried Alana would think it was frivolous, but everyone's had a great response to it."

"Listen, Sheldon, I'm on the Jonathan Darsey case, and we have to be thorough. So I'm going to need to ask you a few questions."

Sheldon tilted his head. "The Jonathan Darsey . . . case?"

Leo quirked his lips. "We're investigating it as a murder. Tentatively."

"Murder! I thought the man was bitten by a dog!"

"We think it's possible someone sicced their dog on him," Leo said.

"My word! Who would . . ."

"Well, that's what I'm investigating. I have to track down Darsey's friends and business associates. I was digging into the property acquisition and your name came up, so I'm here to ask you about it."

Sheldon paled. "Wait . . . you don't think . . . you don't think I would do something like that, do you, Leo?"

"Of course not, Sheldon," Leo said. "I was looking into the property angle and was as surprised as anyone when your name popped up. But I have to follow every lead so I can show I remained unbiased in my investigation. Just a few questions."

"My gosh!" Sheldon replied. "I mean, I wouldn't even have known what the man looked like if his photo hadn't run in the paper after his death. I haven't ever met him. Just heard his name."

"And you said you put in a bid for the property at the last minute?"

He nodded. "Yes, I only started looking at properties within the last week. They might have looked more closely at my bid, but it turned out that they had just inked the deal with Darsey. I was disappointed, but you don't expect to buy the first property you look at. There were a few others I was considering."

"Good, good." Leo jotted down notes. "Just so I can rule you out right away, can you give me an alibi for last Monday afternoon and evening?"

Sheldon's chest puffed. "I was on a date!"

"With Alana?" Leo asked with a smile.

Sheldon's face reddened, but he looked proud. "Yes. We've been going on quite a few dates lately. That day, we were across town at that little Irish pub on the corner for a late lunch. Lots of people saw me there. And, afterwards, Alana and I went bowling."

"I'll confirm with her," Leo said. "And I trust you'll be open to follow-up questions?"

"Absolutely!" Sheldon said. "I have nothing to hide."

CHAPTER 13

*L*eo wandered back into the library looking for Larry, then checked his texts. Larry had sent him a message.

Ran an errand. Meet you back at the station.

Hopefully, the errand had something to do with a breakthrough in the case. Perhaps the man had found something in his research about one of the women Jonathan might have been cheating with?

Leo headed out, relieved that he wouldn't have to listen to Larry on the drive. Plus, it was just about lunchtime, so he might as well take his midday break.

He headed downtown, pulling up just outside Mona's shop. Her car was parked outside, just as he had hoped. A little thrill ran through him. He'd ask her out to lunch—and also take a peek to see how the shop was coming along. Mona, he knew, was starting to get anxious, as the opening date was quickly approaching.

Leo went to the front door and peeked through the glass. She was busying herself with something near the front counter. He tapped on the door, and her head shot up. A grin appeared on her face, and she hurried over to let him in.

"Leo!" she exclaimed happily. "I'm so glad you came by!"

He looked around with a smile, soaking in his surroundings. The antique shelves had all been put up, and the paint colors she had chosen—mostly neutrals in shades of cream and brown—worked well with the rustic look she was going for.

"Whoa," he said. "This place is really coming together!"

"The electrician just left, and everything's in place. I can hardly believe it, but everything is finally, officially ready for me to start stocking shelves!"

"I'm so proud of you," he said. "After a fire, I know a lot of people would have given up. You're amazing."

Mona blushed. "Thanks, Leo. Oh! Come check out this one display I've been working on!" She hurried over to the far side of the shop to show off an enormous bookshelf-like display case. Leo grinned as it came into view. There were cute, cartoonish, wooden honeybees all around the rim of the case.

"I'm guessing this is where Vicki will display her honey treats?" he asked.

"I haven't shown her the cabinet yet. You think she'll like it?"

"Are you kidding? She's going to love it," he said. "Did you make those little bees yourself?"

"That I did. Found an idea for it online."

"Adorable." He glanced back over his shoulder toward the back counter and noticed an enormous bouquet of flowers. "Whoa. What's with the flowers?"

Mona grunted, heading toward the counter. The arrangement was huge. The vase itself was nearly as large as Leo's torso, and the array of pink, white, and red roses seemed to almost gleam in the soft light.

"That would be Larry Simmons," she said, picking up a small card that had evidently come with the roses. "They arrived just a few minutes ago."

Leo took the card.

Congratulations on your success, beautiful! -Larry

Rage built up inside his chest.

Is this why Larry left the station early?

"When did he send these?" Leo asked.

"I imagine he must have called them in after I bumped into him at the station." She shook her head. "Does he know that we're . . . ?" She trailed off as if she weren't quite sure how to finish the sentence.

"He should," Leo muttered. "I can't believe he's really flirting with you."

Her cheeks pinked a little. "He's just being nice."

Agitation tugged at his chest. Why was she trying to defend him? Larry's words churned in his mind. *You know, she and I went out.* He gritted his teeth. He had to ask, or it would eat him alive.

"So, I heard a little rumor," he said.

"Oh?"

"Yeah. Um . . . did you and Larry date at one point?"

She shrugged and shifted uncomfortably. "We went on a couple dates."

"Just casual dates, or were you an item?"

"Well . . . I don't know that we ever really defined it," she said, reaching out to brush one of the flowers. "I mean, we went on . . . maybe two dates? Three at most? It ended when he left for school."

"How did it go?" Leo asked. "Dating Larry, I mean."

She looked like she wanted to melt through the floor. "Fine, I guess. He was a gentleman. Opened my car door for me, that kind of thing. Hey, it must be your lunch break. Want to grab a bite to eat?"

It was an obvious bid to change the subject, but the direction the conversation had taken had opened up a pit of dread in his stomach, and he wanted to talk about anything else. "Absolutely."

Because the shop was located on Main Street, there were plenty of places to eat within walking distance. They settled on a local café that served amazing paninis, and soon they were seated across from one another. He worked hard to put the picture of Larry and Mona dating out of his head.

"I'm so relieved that Chippy got cleared," Mona said. "Are you going to give him a new name, or are you keeping it as Chippy?"

"Hmm. I kind of like Chippy," he said, relaxing into the new topic. Even if Mona and Larry *had* dated—even if they might have *kept* dating if Larry hadn't left for Harvard—that didn't mean Mona was still interested in him.

But why was she trying to avoid the subject?

He swallowed hard and forced his mind to focus on the conversation. Chippy. Was he going to change Chippy's name? He added, "Plus, he definitely responds to the name, so I think I'll keep it as is."

"How are you liking having a dog at your house?"

"Honestly? A lot more than I expected to." He chuckled. "He's a funny dog. Well behaved, although I keep having to kick him out of my bed. He thinks he can sleep with me. Maybe I should get him his own dog bed. I sent Sharon an email, and she told me that Jonathan would always let him sleep with them. So, I guess he thinks that's just what he's supposed to do."

"Aww, looks like you're stuck with him curling up in your bed with you then," she said with a grin.

"Until I fix my bedroom door," he grumbled.

"Aww! That dog loves you," she said. "You really going to give him the boot?"

"Maybe. It wouldn't be so bad, but he sprawls out. I nearly fell out of bed this morning."

She snorted. "Well, I'm just so glad nothing bad happened to him. How's the case coming along?"

"Confusing, honestly," Leo said, his brow furrowing. "Someone clearly assaulted Jonathan and his dog. But why did Jonathan even have the dog? Sharon says Chippy was missing, but not until the day after Jonathan's death."

"Wait . . ." Mona's face scrunched up in concentration. "Did Sharon say exactly when Chippy went missing?"

Leo thought for a moment. "She said she realized he was gone Tuesday morning."

"But Sharon's not an attentive pet owner. What if he really went missing the day of the murder?"

"Well . . ." Leo was surprised he hadn't thought of that. "That could change everything, couldn't it?"

Mona tapped her fingers against the tabletop. "Maybe. What if Jonathan stole Chippy?"

The waiter brought them their sandwiches, and Mona dug in at once. But Leo's mind was still twisting and turning over the case.

He nodded. "Makes sense. Sharon did say Jonathan had been by recently, trying to convince her to hand the dog over. And it sounded like Chippy really loved Jonathan. He would have come right up to him, so it's not like it would have been difficult for Jonathan to swipe the dog."

"The microchip!" Mona exclaimed.

"Yes," said Leo, picking up on her line of thought immediately. "That's why the microchip information was erased the weekend before Jonathan's death. When Jonathan failed to convince Sharon to hand Chippy over, he devised a plan to steal him. The microchip would prove that Chippy was Chippy if Sharon pursued the theft."

"But without the microchip information, Jonathan could claim that he'd just adopted another golden retriever," Mona finished.

"Exactly!"

"Okay, so Jonathan is out walking his dog far away from his home so he's not busted with the stolen dog. Then . . . someone does bump into him and confronts him about stealing the dog?" Mona suggested, taking a bite of her panini.

Leo shook his head slowly. "Well, Magnolia Falls Trail is fairly close to the Darsey estate, actually, where Sharon lives. So maybe Jonathan parked at the trailhead, hiked to the estate, stole Chippy, and was heading back to his car when he was killed? That might be a way to avoid getting caught on security footage. The road to the estate has a huge gate and lots of cameras."

"Does Sharon have an alibi?" Mona asked.

"Yeah—a solid one, in fact. She was hosting a party at her home the entire day of the murder. Plenty of people saw her."

"It'd be odd for him to break into the estate when there were that many people there, but maybe he didn't know she was going to be hosting a party. Or maybe that's why he wore the suit . . . So he could blend in? Okay, so someone else—someone who knew Sharon's dog was missing—saw Jonathan take him, maybe? Or recognized Chippy, at least? Someone who would take offense at Jonathan enough to stab him."

"And then sic another dog on him," Leo said. "It wouldn't have been one of the event attendees, because it was a fancy affair. Not the sort of thing you bring a dog to."

"Do any of your suspects live near the trail?"

"No," Leo said. "But I like this train of thought. It's giving me some ideas."

"Don't work too hard."

"Nah," Leo said, smiling. "Although I'm working from home this afternoon."

"Oh?"

"Well, it's Saturday, so the station's staffed a little lighter anyway. I only went into work because homicide investigations don't stop for the weekend. But Chippy's vet is open every other Saturday. Taking him there in a couple hours to have his stitches checked."

Mona took another bite of her sandwich. "Well, enjoy your afternoon away from Larry, then."

Leo laughed aloud, but hearing Larry's name from Mona put a sour taste in his mouth. "Oh, believe me, I will."

CHAPTER 14

When Leo opened the door, the world's most excited dog greeted him. Chippy jumped for joy, letting out excited little whines, his tail thwacking faster than a hummingbird's wings.

"Come on, let's go out," Leo said, opening the back door. Chippy zoomed past him, and Leo forced himself to stop thinking about Larry and Mona. He was overreacting. This was fine. She probably just felt awkward having a conversation about an ex so early.

Surely she didn't still have feelings for Larry.

Chippy darted from one end of the yard to the other. Leo tossed him a ball for a few minutes before Chippy got bored and started sniffing around the edge of the grass. A minute later, a wet nose nudged Leo's hand. He glanced down. Chippy had brought him a rock. He chuckled and took the rock, patting him on the head. "Good boy. Time to go in."

They went back inside, and he checked the dog's injury. As far as he could tell, it looked good—nearly healed. He rebandaged the stitches and headed upstairs to change out of his uniform. When he returned wearing his oldest pair of jeans and a white T-shirt, Chippy barked as if he thought this was a sign they were going to do something fun.

Leo laughed. "Sorry, Chippy. We're just going to hang out here for a bit before your vet appointment."

Leo tossed Chippy a honey-flavored treat, and Chippy chomped down on it.

"You know, it's kind of nice to come home to a dog," Leo mused, kneeling down.

Chippy ran to Leo and licked his face.

Leo scrambled to his feet and wiped off the dog saliva, snorting. "Now, that I could do without."

The doorbell rang. Chippy barked and raced toward the door.

"Guard dog instincts, huh?" asked Leo. He peered through the peephole.

Ugh. Why's Larry here?

Larry was the last person he wanted to talk to right now.

But it wasn't as though he could pretend he wasn't home. Both his patrol car and personal vehicle were sitting in the driveway. Plus, surely Larry had heard Chippy barking, so Leo clearly wasn't taking the dog for a walk. He glanced down at Chippy, and the dog whined.

"You're telling me." Leo shook his head as he answered the door. "Larry. What's up?"

"What's up, partner?" Larry said, shoving past Leo into the house. "I got something for you." He held up a small, wrapped gift. "Well, for the dog, that is. I figured you probably needed a few things, being a new pet owner and all."

Leo forced a smile. "That's actually nice of you."

"No problem." Larry shoved the wrapped gift into Leo's hands. "Got it from this fancy pet shop that sells specially made collars. Wasn't sure if you were renaming it or not, so I didn't have a tag made. It's a collar and a leash."

"Oh, that's actually perfect," Leo said. "Sharon dropped his old ones by, but they're kind of old and dingy. He deserves something better."

"Well, glad I could be of service," Larry said. "But I'm also here on business. I know you've got the afternoon off, so I hope I'm not intruding?"

"It's fine," Leo said.

It wasn't fine. If Larry wanted to discuss the case, he should have called. Leo's house was his safe haven. But . . . too late now.

"What is it you need? I do have to get Chippy to a vet appointment in a little bit."

"Well, I looked into those names you gave me," Larry began. "I gathered some preliminary information on the internet, then decided to go visit the women myself."

Leo nodded approvingly, though, in truth, he was a little alarmed. Had Larry gone and accused every single woman of murder? Did he know any other way to investigate a case? "How did that go?"

"I was able to speak to all five of them. One of them, Sharon's hairdresser, told me she's never even met Jonathan. The other four knew him—people he's worked with or old family friends. But they *all* denied having an affair with him. Frankly, they all seemed pretty insulted that Sharon would accuse them of such a thing. I called the judge who oversaw the divorce and even managed to get in touch with Jonathan's old divorce lawyer too. Couldn't find any sign that Sharon had accused Jonathan of having an affair during the divorce."

"Really?" Leo asked, reaching down to scratch Chippy's head. "You'd think something like that would have helped her out in the divorce."

"My thoughts exactly," Larry said. "So, why bring it up now? Unless it was some sort of red herring."

"Let's look more into Sharon." Leo frowned. "I don't like that she could be lying to us about something like that. It looks like she's trying to pass the blame."

"Alibi or no, she's rich," Larry said. "Maybe she hired someone? I mean, she fought to get the man's dog, for crying out loud. And, if she's letting you keep the dog, it doesn't sound like she was particularly fond of the thing."

Leo nodded slowly. "Definitely a possibility. We'll have to look into it more." If Sharon were involved, then there was no reason to think she was telling the truth about when Chippy went missing—which opened up a whole host of possibilities.

"Seems like Jonathan must have swiped Chippy," Leo added. "Maybe that sent Sharon over the edge? She seemed to have been insulted by Jonathan's affection for the dog and lack of affection toward her. Maybe that was her plan? Send someone after Jonathan to sic a dog on him to make it look like Chippy hurt him? It would be a really twisted form of revenge—get your ex-husband murdered and frame the dog he loved so much? I mean, that's probably a bit of a stretch."

"Sounds like something out of a cheesy novel," Larry said.

"Truth is stranger than fiction sometimes."

Then Larry shook his head. "What if we're making this too complicated? If Jonathan stole Chippy . . . maybe Chippy just got in a fight with another dog in the woods and Jonathan got in the way."

"But the stab wounds?" Leo asked.

With a shrug, Larry said, "Maybe the other dog's owner got involved too. I hate to break it to you, but if the owner says they stabbed in self-defense and that the dog bit of its own accord, there's not much we can do aside from putting down the dog. They didn't have a legal responsibility to stop and help Darsey out. Darsey's relatives could sue them in civil court for not controlling their dog, but it'd be hard to make any criminal charges stick."

"There's more than that. I'm sure of it. But we'll figure it out. I've got to admit, I'm pretty impressed with your detective work," Leo said in spite of himself, pleasantly surprised by all Larry had gotten done that day.

"Well, I *have* been doing this for a while."

"Yeah, yeah, yeah." Leo thought back to his conversation with Mona. And the flowers Larry had sent. No, he wouldn't get too friendly with Larry just yet. "Hey, man, I need to talk to you about something."

Larry raised a brow. "Oh?"

"It's personal."

"Shoot. What's bugging you?"

"Well, honestly, *you*." Leo crossed his arms. "Man, what are you doing sending a woman flowers when I'm clearly seeing her?"

Larry pursed his lips. "Saw that, did you?"

"Yeah, I did. And you keep making weird comments about Mona in front of me. It's not cool, Larry."

"So, are you two . . . like . . . official?"

Leo paused. It wasn't exactly a conversation he and Mona had broached yet. "Well, we've only just started dating."

"How many dates have you been on, exactly?"

"Well, I guess . . . two . . . three if you count lunch today."

"Are you counting the one where you found a dead body? Not exactly romantic."

Leo wasn't about to reveal that the second date had been an impromptu night in taking care of Chippy and making jam. "That's beside the point, Larry. You and I are supposed to be partners. And you going behind my back—"

"I think you're overreacting," Larry said, trying to wave it off. "The girl is opening up a shop downtown. It's kind of a big deal. All I did was send her some congratulatory flowers."

"Would you do that for anyone else?"

Larry winked at him. "If they looked like her, I sure would."

"Okay, out," Leo said, opening the front door. "It was good talking to you, Larry. Now, if you'll excuse me, I've got to get my dog to the vet."

"See you tomorrow, partner," Larry called on his way out, and Leo slammed the door behind him.

Leo glanced down at Chippy. The dog seemed to be wearing a matching expression of annoyance. He sighed and picked up the wrapped gift. "I suppose it was nice of him to bring this." But when he opened the package, he frowned. The collar and leash were . . . *glittering*. Every inch was bright blue and bedazzled.

"Seriously?" he demanded, picking up a collar that boasted a gold star, like an officer's uniform. Leo rolled his eyes at the gaudy design. "Ugh . . . would it be rude if I didn't use it? It's so stupid looking."

But it was better than the collar that smelled like wet dog and mud.

"I guess this'll have to do for now," he said as he put the collar on Chippy. "Sorry."

They headed out the door, and Leo cringed. The leash and collar seemed even flashier in the sunlight.

He looked up in horror as a patrol car slowed in front of his house. Ann was driving, and she rolled down the window.

"Oh my gosh! Nice! Wait until the guys hear about this!" she called, cackling before speeding off.

Leo threw a hand in the air. "Aww, forget you, Ann!" he shouted.

He felt like one of those prima donnas who take their little purse dogs to have their nails done.

He glanced down at Chippy. "After the vet appointment, we're stopping by the pet store to get you a new collar."

CHAPTER 15

*L*eo awoke Monday morning to a sloppy, wet kiss from Chippy. "Ah! I told you to stop doing that!" Leo yelped, rolling over.

He wiped off his face and blinked his eyes open. Chippy was still wearing the shimmering police-themed collar. The pet store had been closed due to a plumbing issue.

"I think Larry might have gotten that stupid thing to embarrass me on purpose," Leo muttered, and Chippy almost seemed to nod in agreement.

His phone buzzed with a text from his sister. *Tonight, 7:00, my place, double date.*

This must be the grand date Vicki was planning. He chuckled and texted back a GIF of a thumbs-up, then hurried to get ready and run through the Chippy-related chores. As he grabbed his coffee thermos, he checked the time. He was three minutes late.

He didn't make a habit of being late.

He flung the door open and came face-to-face with Aunt Bee, her fist raised as though she'd been about to knock.

"Well, that was excellent timing, Leo," she said from behind a new pair of bright-red frames.

"Looking good, Aunt Bee," Leo said with a wink.

She touched her new glasses and grinned. "About time I got

these," she warbled. "Can hardly get through a Coupon Clippers meeting without squinting at my notes and straining these old eyes of mine."

"What are you doing here? Not that it isn't always great to see you." Time to accept his fate: he was going to be late.

He stepped aside, allowing Aunt Bee to come in. Chippy danced right up to her, sniffed her hands, and wagged his tail approvingly before returning to his dog bowl.

Aunt Bee sighed with dramatic flair. "I'm here because I'm worried!" she cried. "About my friend."

"Who? Sheldon?" Leo asked.

"Exactly!" she yelped. "He told me about your little meeting at the library, and I am very upset by the whole thing! I don't want to see a nice man like Sheldon get in trouble. Do you think someone might accuse him of hurting Jonathan Darsey just because he's buying that piece of property?"

"I doubt it, Aunt Bee," Leo said. "But don't worry; I'm heading up the case. It's my job to exhaust every lead. I don't believe for a second that Sheldon would hurt a fly. But I still had to talk to him. I'm not investigating Sheldon, or anything like that. Even though I didn't think he hurt Darsey, he still might have stumbled on useful information in the course of buying the property."

Aunt Bee nodded, but she still seemed quite worried. "Have you looked into Mr. Bonds?"

Mr. Who? "James Bonds?" he asked with a smirk.

"Honestly, Leo!" she exclaimed. "Nick Bonds! He was Jonathan Darsey's old business partner until they had a falling out."

He blinked at her. "How . . . do *you* know that? Nothing like that has come up in my research."

"I've been living in this town since I was a little girl," she said with a wink. "I know all the gossip from here to Pigeon Hollow, dear."

Leo took a moment to pull up the man's name online. Sure enough, he was able to sift through his social media pages to find that he had, indeed, once worked alongside Jonathan Darsey. There wasn't much about their supposed falling out, but Aunt Bee was certain of her intel.

"Well, I'll go speak to him this morning," Leo said. It would be the perfect excuse for his tardiness.

"Wonderful! I'm coming with you," Aunt Bee trilled. Before Leo could protest, she was already out the door and halfway to his patrol car.

"Um! Aunt Bee!" Leo called. He glanced down at Chippy, who seemed to almost shrug at him. "I'll see you later, buddy."

By the time he locked the house and caught up with her, she was standing by the passenger-side door, waiting for him to let her in.

"Aunt Bee, I'm going to have to insist that you stay behind. I can't be taking you all over town interviewing potential murder suspects."

"Oh, honey," she said, shaking her head. "You and I both know how this conversation is going to end, so why don't you skip the part where you waste time. Go ahead and be a gentleman and open the door for me."

The confidence in her voice was unflappable, and the next thing Leo knew, he was driving in his patrol car with Aunt Bee chattering away in the passenger seat.

"And then my sister says to me . . . Do you want to hear what she says to me? She says she got herself a new boyfriend! Goodness! The woman is rapidly approaching her mid-seventies, and she's off dating some gold-digging fortysomething! She knows it, too! She knows exactly what these men in her life are up to, yet she goes along with it! Honestly, if she'd actually stuck around and wasn't off gallivanting in a different town every month, she might have wound up with Nick Bonds."

"Why do you say that?" Leo asked with a slight chuckle.

"Why, he's a money-hungry creep," Aunt Bee insisted. "Just look at the way he is with Sharon. At least she's close to his own age. He left his first wife to chase an older, rich woman years ago. No wonder his son went to jail. Bonds was so focused on skirt-chasing he wasn't around to be a real parent. He thought that paying for that private school would be enough, but kids need quality time!"

Leo raised a brow. "Pardon? Go back to the part about Sharon."

"Well, honey, don't you know?" Aunt Bee asked. "They're getting married next June. They just had their engagement party on Monday."

He slammed on his brakes, pulling into the nearest parking lot. Then he paused, took a breath, and looked directly at Aunt Bee. "Sharon, as in Jonathan Darsey's ex-wife Sharon?"

"That's exactly who I mean," Aunt Bee. "Don't you read the paper? They had their engagement announcement in there."

Well, *that* certainly changed the way he needed to approach things. He pulled out his phone and began doing a bit of research online.

"What are you doing?" Aunt Bee asked. "Aren't we going to speak with Nick Bonds?"

"Yes, but I don't want to go in blind without knowing all of the facts," he said. "Ah . . . interesting . . . Sharon tried telling me that Jonathan had been having a bunch of affairs. When Larry got back from interviewing all the women Sharon mentioned Jonathan had been seeing , he told me that every last one outright denied it. One had never even met Jonathan. I think Sharon was blowing smoke. *Sharon* was the one having an affair."

"What did you find?"

"A post from a year and a half ago on Jonathan Darsey's social media page from right around the time Sharon filed for divorce: him ranting about his soon-to-be ex-wife, calling her a cheating . . . I'll spare you the details of the language he chose to use. But look who came to her defense on the post." He showed his phone to her.

She squinted through her new glasses. "Nick Bonds."

"Exactly. And then Darsey fires back and calls Bonds a traitor before they both stop commenting on the post." He thought for a moment. "I'm going to make a quick stop at the courthouse, Aunt Bee, before we go speak to Nick."

The county courthouse was only a few minutes away. The place was already bustling with lawyers. The two of them remained in the car for several minutes, watching the front steps of the building.

"What are we waiting for?" Aunt Bee asked curiously.

"A fellow by the name of Monroe Gains," he said. "Sharon's divorce lawyer. I spoke to him briefly over the phone the other day, but he wasn't very helpful. But he did mention he had a court hearing this morning. I'm going to try to catch him before . . . Wait, there he is!

Stay here." Leo jumped out of the patrol car and hurried to intercept an older man in a fine suit.

"Hey, Monroe," Leo said casually.

The man frowned. "Ah, Detective Lawson . . . I'm running a tad late, if you don't mind."

"Oh, then I'll make this quick," Leo said, giving the man the stink eye to let him know he wasn't messing around.

The lawyer frowned, then straightened. "All right, fine. What do you need?"

"Nick Bonds. I've come to learn that he and Sharon had been having an affair when you were representing her in the divorce," Leo said confidently. He didn't *really* know this for sure, but he wanted to project confidence.

Monroe glared at him. "Look, I'm not at liberty to discuss private information."

"Of course," Leo said. "I'm not asking about your client, Sharon, though. I want to know about Nick."

"I've never represented Nick," Monroe said. "I don't know—"

"Sharon got just about everything in the divorce," Leo said. "Despite taking up with Jonathan's business partner. You must be an excellent attorney."

"I thought you were asking about Nick?"

"I'm getting to that. Tell me, how do you know him?" Leo asked. "You do know him, don't you?"

Monroe hesitated. "You know what? I really don't have time for this." He tried to step around Leo, but Leo blocked his path.

"Come on, Monroe. A man is dead. And it's looking like you might have conspired with Sharon and Nick to take everything from him."

"Conspired!" Monroe sputtered. "You're out of your mind. I had nothing to do with this."

"Are you sure? Are you sure, Monroe?" Leo asked. "Because what I've uncovered isn't looking good."

Monroe stiffened, appearing quite flustered. Frankly, Leo had just been casting a line and hoping he'd bite.

"I'm certain!" Monroe snapped. "Fine. You're going to be a thorn in my side, aren't you? Nick Bonds was most certainly having an affair with Sharon, but you didn't hear that from me."

"Interesting. What else you got for me, Monroe?"

"I can tell you that this was the easiest divorce case I've ever worked," Monroe said. "Jonathan was a fool who put just about everything in his wife's name, and Sharon . . . hinted . . . to me that Nick had told her to convince Jonathan to do it. It was painfully obvious that the affair had been going on for a long time. They planned it carefully, though. And Jonathan didn't fight back because Sharon threatened to go public with evidence that he'd hit her. Sharon got Jonathan's half of just about all of the business ventures, so Sharon was able to turn everything over to Nick. She still has half of everything in her name, but Nick might as well own a hundred percent of the businesses he and Jonathan built together. But don't go feeling sorry for Jonathan Darsey. He really did hit Sharon when he got drunk."

"Thank you, Monroe," Leo said, finally stepping aside.

Monroe pointed a finger at Leo. "Don't you dare show up here again harassing me about a case. You could get me in serious deep water."

Leo merely nodded and departed without saying another word. Once he was back in the car with Aunt Bee, he filled her in before they made their way to Nick Bonds's home. Much to Leo's surprise, there was a familiar-looking vehicle sitting out front. "That . . . that's Larry's car," he said. "No way that dope beat me to Nick Bonds."

"Well, Leo, dear . . . he does have a Harvard education," Aunt Bee said. "Larry might be obnoxious, but he knows what he's doing."

Leo huffed and stepped out of the car just as Larry exited the home alongside Nick Bonds and a younger man.

Larry looked up and made eye contact with Leo. He nodded approvingly and spoke again to Nick for a moment before heading toward the patrol car. The two men disappeared back inside the house.

"What's up, partner?" Larry called. "What are you doing here?"

"I could ask you the same question." Leo strode toward Larry, Aunt Bee right on his heels. "You found out about Sharon and Nick before I did?"

Larry grinned. "It's not a competition, Leo. We're partners, remember?"

"Right," Leo said, aggravated. "Partners. Did you learn anything?"

"Nothing I didn't already know," Larry said. "I'll fill you in later. Gotta get back to the station."

Leo stood there, completely dumbfounded, as Larry drove off.

CHAPTER 16

A long stretch of cars lined Aunt Bee's street. One of her neighbors must be having some kind of gathering, Leo mused. He parked about a block away to drop her off.

Aunt Bee stepped out of the patrol car, glasses perched carefully on her nose as she peered at the road. She huffed. "Why wasn't I invited?"

Loud hip-hop music streamed from a nearby yard, and he chuckled at the thought of Aunt Bee strutting around at a lunchtime barbeque clearly meant for college kids.

"I have no idea," Leo said. "You seem like a real party animal, Aunt Bee."

She laughed and hooked her arm through his. "You are too sweet, walking an old lady home."

"I try." He glanced up past the line of houses toward the wooded hills. "I like your neighborhood."

"I do too," Aunt Bee said. "Now, what's bothering you?"

He let out a long sigh. He definitely wasn't going to have a heart-to-heart with Aunt Bee about Mona, so he said, "I really don't know what to think about Larry Simmons. Sometimes he's a straight shooter. Doing real detective work. I mean, he found out about Nick Bonds before I did. Then he has days when he's getting into people's faces, just outright accusing people of murder. It's like he forgets how to behave some days."

"Some people are just like that," she said. "Especially people like Larry Simmons who think they have something to prove."

"You think Larry believes he has something to prove? He's the town prodigy." Leo chuckled at the idea that Larry could possibly be the self-conscious type.

"Of course he does!" Aunt Bee said, smacking Leo's arm. "Can you imagine the pressure he's under? All that attention after he got that acceptance letter. People keep waiting for him to do something big. So he feels like he's got to act like he already has."

Leo hadn't thought about it that way. A part of him almost felt bad for Larry. Almost. "Maybe," he said.

The sun dipped behind the trees as they approached Aunt Bee's house. When they turned onto Aunt Bee's street, they saw it was lined with cars just like the rest of the neighborhood.

"Ah, so those are the partygoers," Leo said, looking at a house in the cul-de-sac. "Can't believe your neighbors didn't invite you."

"No one wants an old lady ruining the mood, I suppose," Aunt Bee said. "Plus, the last time I got an invite to one of those kid's get-togethers, my sister tagged along and wore a two-piece...and it wasn't even a pool party."

Leo had to concentrate very hard not to picture that. "Oh, wow," Leo said under his breath, trying not to laugh at the thought.

The stars were just starting to come out when Leo heard a faint growl. Glancing up, he spied a golden retriever sniffing around the yard, moving abruptly as if it were agitated.

"Chippy?" Leo asked, but he knew immediately that he was dead wrong.

The dog looked up at him and Aunt Bee, a rather manic look in its eyes. It growled and snarled, showing its teeth.

"Oh my!" Aunt Bee yelped in surprise. "Where did that dog come from?"

The dog stepped out of her yard and onto the sidewalk, its teeth still exposed. But now that the dog was out in the road, Leo could see it more clearly. It was covered in mud and dried blood . . . and definitely missing a tooth.

"Uh-oh . . ." Leo reached for his gun, only to realize he'd left it in the patrol car.

The music playing at the barbeque changed, giving way to a faster rap song punctuated with banging noises.

Aunt Bee squeaked as the dog started barking madly. Then it hurtled toward them.

"Ah!" Aunt Bee screamed loudly. "Help!"

Leo wasn't about to let his girlfriend's great aunt get mauled by a dog, but the retriever was on them in an instant, and it was clear its intentions were far from friendly. Leo shoved Aunt Bee out of the way, and his heart lurched to see the woman tumble into a nearby bush.

At least this, for the time being, seemed to get her out of harm's way, but the dog turned on Leo, its jaws closing on his calf. Beneath the adrenaline, Leo could vaguely tell he was in pain, but it hadn't really kicked in yet. He hollered, "Get off me, you mutt!"

He rolled over, the dog still latched onto his calf.

"Bad dog!" Aunt Bee shouted.

She'd stood up and was now repeatedly beaning the dog with her pocketbook. "Let go! Bad dog! Bad dog!"

"Aunt Bee—get to the house!" Leo demanded, worried the dog would turn on her.

"Bad dog!" she kept yelling, smacking the retriever. She swung blindly, inadvertently smashing Leo over the head.

"Ah! What do you got in there . . . bricks?" he shouted, now grabbing the dog around the head.

The dog snarled and let go. Much to Leo's relief, his grip on the dog was strong enough to prevent a second bite, despite the retriever's thrashing.

By this point, Aunt Bee's shouts had alerted the neighbors, and a group of frat boys came pouring out into the street.

"Holy cow! Roger, come here! This cop is getting attacked by a dog!" someone shouted, and a swarm of guys in tank tops and oversized sunglasses—despite the cool autumn weather—all crowded around, yanking the aggravated dog off Leo.

"Thanks," Leo said, panting, rubbing the side of his head where Aunt Bee's pocketbook had collided with his skull.

The dog was losing its mind, but one of the young men held its jaw shut while another grabbed it from behind to keep it still.

"Someone call an ambulance for this guy," someone said.

"Yo, I think I got a muzzle in the house from when I was fostering a dog that bit," another added. "Hold up, Ms. Bee, I'll be right back." He darted off.

Leo wound up having to sit. He rolled up his pant leg to take a look at his injury and cringed at the blood dripping down his leg. "Geez! I've probably got rabies or something!"

"Hold on," Aunt Bee said, looking back toward the house. "Roger, go turn off that music!"

A college-aged guy ran off, and a few moments later, the loud music stopped. The dog calmed almost immediately, though it was still fidgety and trembling. It even cooperated when Roger arrived back with the muzzle.

"Aunt Bee, how did you know the music was bothering him?" Leo asked from his spot on the ground.

An ambulance pulled up alongside them, and relief flooded him. Now that the threat was over, searing pain pulsed in his leg. He was looking forward to some pain medicine.

"I've seen what a dog with rabies looks like," Aunt Bee said. "This dog isn't crazy. It was scared. It got more agitated when the music made that *pop-pop* sound."

"Oh, yeah," Roger said as the paramedics came hurrying over. "That song's got gunshots in the background. It's an old rap mix."

The dog kept whining. After a moment, it lay down on the sidewalk near Leo, crying.

"Stupid dog," Leo muttered. "Aunt Bee, would you mind giving my friend Denise a call? She's in my contact list." Leo handed up his cell phone. "Tell her Leo needs her out this way."

"Of course!" Aunt Bee warbled, taking the phone and stepping aside to make the call.

The dog was completely calm now, though it was panting as if its little outburst had drained it of energy.

"Stupid dog," Leo said again.

A paramedic examined the bite mark. "I'll clean this out," she said, "and it'll hurt. But I don't think you need stitches, so no need to transport you by ambulance unless you'd prefer an ER doc check you out."

"I'd rather avoid the bill," said Leo.

The paramedic nodded. "You should call your doctor and get antibiotics, though."

"Great, thanks," replied Leo. "Any chance of numbing it first?"

"Mmm, I could give you an injection, but you may find it difficult to walk until it wears off."

So much for that. "Just clean it," he said through gritted teeth.

She was right. It hurt like the dickens.

Through the haze of pain, he watched the dog curl up next to Aunt Bee's neighbor, Roger. The thing seemed to be taking a liking to him.

When the bite had been cleaned and bandaged, Leo sent the paramedics on their way.

"Why did it get so freaked out?" Leo huffed.

Roger shrugged, rubbing the dog's ears. "Beats me," he said. "Doesn't seem vicious now, does it?"

Leo studied the dog. It *had* to be the one that had killed Darsey. It was missing a tooth and had clearly exhibited aggression.

But why?

It whimpered again and cuddled up closer to Roger, and Leo felt sick to his stomach. As soon as Denise confirmed that this was their killer dog, it would surely have to be put down.

His thoughts raced as Roger spoke to the dog in soothing tones.

Why had the dog attacked Darsey? And had someone intentionally provoked it to kill?

Then he glanced at his phone, and all thoughts of the case vanished from his mind. His stomach sank.

He'd gotten a text from Mona: *Hey, Leo, I'm really sorry about this, but I think it's better if we just stay friends.*

CHAPTER 17

"*M*orning, Chippy," Leo said as he limped out of the bathroom. He rubbed his bleary eyes.

What a terrible week. He was *still* stuck working with Larry Simpleton Simmons, the case wasn't making sense, and he'd lost his chance with the girl of his dreams.

He hadn't slept well the night before, between the pain in his leg and the way his thoughts kept circling back to Mona. *Oh no. I forgot to tell Vicki that we weren't coming on the double date. We stood her up.*

But, then again, Mona had probably told her.

Why had Mona changed her mind so quickly? Did she just not feel the same way he did? Did she still have feelings for Larry? The thought made him sick to his stomach.

He let Chippy run around in the yard for a while, then refilled the kibble bowl and fixed himself a cup of coffee. He had to leave shortly to meet Larry at a café.

Compartmentalize. Focus on the case.

He'd try his best.

Denise had called him the evening before and confirmed that the other retriever—who Leo had nicknamed Cujo—was definitely the dog that had killed Darsey. "We'll have to turn it over to animal control to be put down," she'd said.

"Where is it right now?" he asked.

"I've got him in a kennel here at the morgue," she replied.

"Would you mind sitting on that information for me?" he asked. "Tell anyone who asks that you haven't finished processing his bite marks yet? I'm concerned there may be something bigger going on, and I don't want to risk destroying any evidence."

Plus, despite the pain in his leg, he couldn't help it—he wanted to give the dog a stay of execution. It had looked so sad after it calmed down.

"Sure," she said, sounding skeptical. "I mean, he's been perfectly sweet and all, but the forensics don't lie."

"Just give me a day or two."

So, now, he had to figure out if there really was *something bigger* going on, before they killed the dog. And he didn't have much time.

Leo dragged himself out the door. A few minutes later, he arrived at the café. Larry was already there, and he waved at Leo from a window seat. Leo sighed as he made his way inside.

Don't think about Mona. Don't think about Mona.

"What's up, Leo?" Larry called, waving him over.

Leo sat down across from Larry in the booth. "Morning."

"Heard you had a rough evening," Larry said. "Looks like you're still limping."

"Yeah, not one of my proudest moments," Leo admitted. "So, I got a call from Denise last night. Cujo was a match. Which means we found the dog that killed Jonathan. But I asked her to sit on that, because there's something weird going on. The dog looks *just* like Chippy."

"You think that's not a coincidence?" Larry asked.

"There's no way. Something more happened that day. I just don't know what. I have a feeling that Nick Bonds is somehow involved. Can we go over your interview with him again? He really didn't say anything except for admitting to the affair?"

"I mean, he was cooperative and all," Larry said. "But I don't think he knew anything. Nothing of value to the case, at least."

"Two dogs—two dogs who look a lot alike. And something was up with the dog from last night," Leo mused.

"You're just saying that because it bit you."

"It doesn't have rabies or anything," Leo said. "And golden retrievers aren't exactly known to be violent dogs. Plus, once the music stopped, the dog calmed down. It was aggressive, sure, but it was like it was more scared than anything."

"Maybe the dog was abused or something," Larry suggested.

"By whom?"

"Jonathan? I mean, it did attack him."

"Everyone's said how much Jonathan loved Chippy. He was an animal lover. No way he beat up another dog," Leo said.

"Well, it happened in the middle of the woods," Larry said. "Doubt there was any loud music out that way to freak him out."

"Maybe a gunshot? What if someone was hunting illegally, and the shot freaked out Cujo?"

The server arrived to take their order. Leo ordered himself a light breakfast—two eggs, a piece of toast, and two strips of bacon. Larry, on the other hand, ordered a full breakfast platter and a side of French toast. Leo shook his head, trying to imagine going into work after eating the amount of food Larry had just ordered. It would send him into a full-blown food coma.

Once the server left, Leo turned his attention back to the case. "Hey, let me ask you something. How did you make the connection between Nick Bonds and Jonathan Darsey? During my initial research, I didn't find anything about Nick."

Larry shifted a bit in his seat. "Oh, you know, just heavy research. Kept digging into Darsey, and eventually Bonds popped up."

Leo stared him down for a moment. His partner was hiding something. But he wouldn't let on that he knew. "Good job. Impressive work, as much as I hate to admit it."

Over breakfast, they discussed a few possible angles, but Leo was starting to feel like they'd hit a brick wall.

Would they ever find out what exactly had happened to Jonathan Darsey?

"I got to say, man, I'm kind of at a loss about what to do next," Larry said.

"Aren't you supposed to be the supercop?" Leo jeered.

Larry crossed his arms. "Usually, I am. But we have nothing. I mean, really. We found the dog that killed Darsey. Isn't that enough?"

"We'll figure it out," Leo said. "Maybe we're missing something. Now that we have more information—now that we've identified the canine culprit—let's go and talk to some of our potential suspects again."

Larry nodded in agreement. "Sounds like a plan."

First, they reinterviewed Kirk from the Go Green group, but he wasn't helpful. "Do you have a dog, by any chance?" asked Leo.

Kirk shook his head. "No, I've always been more of a cat person. I have two cats right now."

When they left, Leo double-checked that information with phone calls to a couple of people who had known Kirk a long time, plus a brief skim of Kirk's social media history.

"Seems like a dead end," he finally said to Larry. On to the next person. Though Nick seemed like the most promising lead, he decided to go to Sheldon's first.

He pulled onto Sheldon's street.

"Oh, I grew up around here. So, who is this guy we're going to see?" Larry asked with an uninterested yawn.

"The guy buying the property that Darsey was going to build that factory on."

"You think he could have been the one who stabbed Darsey?" Larry asked.

"Definitely not," Leo said. "But he's an old-timer who knows just about everyone around here. He might be able to tell us more about Nick Bonds. He didn't know Darsey, but Bonds grew up in Magnolia Falls."

"Oh," Larry said, squirming.

Leo and Larry headed to the door, and Leo rang the bell. Sheldon swung the door open, smiling brightly.

"Hey, Leo. Come on in. Who's your friend?"

They entered Sheldon's home, and Leo smiled. "Thanks, Sheldon. This is my partner, Larry—"

"Ah! Larry Simmons!" Sheldon said, and Leo noticed that Larry seemed suddenly anxious.

"Oh, good, you know each other," Leo said.

"Why, sure." Sheldon nodded. "You're the Harvard boy. You grew up one street over."

"Yes, that's me." Larry grimaced.

"What can I do for you two?" Sheldon asked, sinking down into a recliner.

"Well, I don't know if you've heard, but we found the dog that bit Darsey," Leo said, taking a seat on a couch across from Sheldon.

"I heard." Sheldon chuckled. "Bee told the Coupon Clippers about it!"

"Wonderful," Leo grumbled. "Glad to know I can provide you all with a bit of entertainment."

"Your leg okay?" Sheldon asked.

"It's been better," Leo said. "But I'll be fine. I was wondering if you could tell us anything about Nick Bonds."

Sheldon stared at Leo awkwardly for a moment. "What are you asking me for?" He waved a hand in Larry's direction. "Larry and Nick's boy, Albert, have been buddies since elementary school. They went to private school together. Oh, I remember seeing Albert and Larry running around—riding their bikes and causing trouble."

Leo turned abruptly toward Larry. "You didn't mention that you were friends with Nick Bonds's son."

Larry shrugged his shoulders. "Didn't think it was worth mentioning."

Leo raised his voice. "If it wasn't anything, then why didn't you tell me the real reason you knew about Nick Bonds? If you're an old family friend, you would've known Darsey and Bonds were old partners, am I right? Why write it off like you'd just done some research?"

Larry shot Leo a look of irritation. "Look, man, I knew how it would seem. Nick's son, Albert . . . he and I have been friends since we were kids. Sharon and I talked the other day, and she asked me to talk to Nick. Make sure everything was okay. She was . . . worried . . . that Nick might have had something to do with Darsey's death. But I looked into it. Everything's fine."

"Are you serious?" Leo snapped.

"Should I leave?" Sheldon held up both his hands.

"No!" both detectives shouted at once.

Sheldon sank down into his seat.

"You're telling me one of our suspects gave you a legitimate lead and you didn't share it with me?" Leo asked.

"She just asked me to go talk to Nick!" Larry stood, his voice growing louder. "And I did. Nick didn't have anything to do with what happened to Darsey."

"Why do you think that? Because he told you so?" Leo demanded. "Your integrity on this case is compromised if you're friends with a suspect's kid!"

Larry waved a hand toward Sheldon. "It's a small town! You're friends with one of the suspects!"

Leo stood up as well. "Yeah, but I didn't hide that fact from you!"

Sheldon's brow frumpled. "I'm a suspect?"

"No! Hush, Sheldon!" Leo pointed a finger at Larry. "You've been acting weird through this entire case. And now I know why! I can see that I'm going to have to look into the Bonds family myself."

"Nick wouldn't kill Darsey!" Larry snapped.

"Just because you're friends with his kid doesn't mean anything," Leo said, crossing his arms. "I cannot believe you, Larry. You really think Nick wouldn't hurt Jonathan? Think about it. He burned Jonathan bad. Real bad. He already weaseled his way into taking both the man's wife and his business. It makes sense that the two men would get into it. Or maybe it was revenge, or a preemptive strike. Darsey really was abusive. Maybe Nick was afraid he'd come after Sharon."

"That still doesn't explain the stupid dog!" Larry shouted. "Nick doesn't even like dogs. Why would he have your little Cujo buddy?"

"I don't know!" Leo snapped. He took a deep breath. "Look, we're not getting anywhere shouting at each other like this."

"No, you two really aren't," Sheldon said. "Do you need me for anything else?"

"We'll get out of your hair." Leo sighed. "Sorry about all the commotion."

They stalked out of Sheldon's house, not looking directly at each other.

"Why don't you just drop me off at my patrol car?" Larry suggested. "I'll go back to the station and see if I can . . . find out anything about Bonds that I don't know."

"Sounds good," Leo said, happy for Larry to leave his presence.

As soon as he dropped Larry off, his phone rang.

It was Mona.

CHAPTER 18

*L*eo pulled into the parking lot, his tires screeching. Mona had begged him to come to the store immediately. She'd said it was an emergency.

Was she in trouble? His heart pounded as he jumped out of the car. She ran out to meet him, waving a flier.

"What is it?" Leo asked, meeting her halfway. "Are you hurt?"

"A missing dog poster!" she exclaimed breathlessly, handing the paper to him. "I'm fine."

Leo glanced at the flier and saw Cujo staring back at him. He frowned, and his heart slowly returned to its normal speed. "So, someone does own that dog. Thought it was a stray."

"Read the bottom."

Leo skimmed down. *Missing Dog. Answers to Tango. Do not approach —Tango frightens easily.*

"No kidding," he muttered. "I'm guessing Aunt Bee told you about what happened with this dog yesterday?"

"Yeah . . ." She scuffed her toe against the sidewalk. "I was so sorry to hear, especially after . . . well . . . but . . . well, I know why the dog attacked you!"

"Oh?" Leo frowned. How could she possibly know that?

"Tango's owner came into my shop just a little bit ago asking if he could put up a poster. Someone stole his dog from his yard on Monday. I told him you'd call him," she said. "Tango is a marine!"

"What? The dog?"

"Yeah. His owner was a marine, and the dog served with him overseas. The dog attacked you because of the loud music; he's got PTSD!" she exclaimed. "The owner is worried about what's going to happen to his dog."

The pieces clicked into place. "That makes a lot of sense. The rap music Bee's neighbors were playing had gunshots in the background. The dog must have gone after me because of his training. He thought I was a threat."

"So, why did he attack Darsey?" Mona asked.

"I'm not sure," Leo said. "But I'm going to find out." He called the number on the flier. The man who answered sounded beyond relieved to hear that the dog had been found.

"I'm at Jammin' Honey right now," said Leo. "Could you come meet me here?"

"I'll be there in ten minutes," the owner replied.

Leo hung up, and he and Mona locked eyes for an awkward moment.

"Um," she said, "why don't you come inside?"

He followed her into the store, which smelled like new paint. Crates of merchandise sat on the counter, waiting to be unpacked.

"It looks great, Mona," he said softly.

Her eyes widened when she looked at him. She'd never looked so beautiful. His heart caught in his throat.

But he'd respect her decision. And she'd decided to just be friends.

They started speaking at the same time, then fell silent.

When Mona waited for him to continue, he said, "Listen, I understand that you don't feel the same way about me. We can just be friends. Just give me some time to get used to it, okay?"

"Leo, it's—"

There was a tapping on the door, and a young man peered through the window. He was leaning on a cane and had two prosthetic legs.

"That him?" Leo asked Mona.

She nodded, her lips pursed, setting aside whatever she'd been about to say.

Leo went to answer the door.

"Detective Lawson?" the man asked, his eyes a bit frightened. "You got my dog? Right? You got Tango?"

"I don't have him here," Leo said, opening the door wider. "Come on in and have a seat. We need to talk about Tango."

"Is he hurt? Is he okay?" the man asked as he came inside. Mona pulled up some chairs for them, and Leo sat down across from the man. He couldn't be a day over twenty-one.

"So, you're Tango's owner?" Leo asked. "Private Elijah Thompson, right?" His phone rang. Vicki was calling. He ignored it.

"That's me," Elijah said. "Tango's been missing for about a week now. Someone stole him right out of my yard! Is he okay?"

"He's just fine."

Elijah's shoulders relaxed.

Now came the bad news. "But Tango is in a bit of trouble. I hate to tell you this, but your dog killed a man."

Elijah's eyes widened, and his entire demeanor changed, as if he were sinking into a shell of himself. "What's going to happen to him?" he asked dully. "They're going to make me put him down, aren't they?"

"I'm not sure just yet. We're still trying to piece together exactly what happened. Can you tell me more about Tango?"

"He was one of the sentries for our unit," Elijah explained. "Military guard dog. Well trained. Not another one like him. He was my buddy, you know? Good dog. Really good dog. Saved my life."

"He saved your life?" Leo asked, glancing at Mona.

"Yeah, that dog's got more medals than my commanding officer. There was . . . an air strike . . ." Elijah tapped his cane against his bionic legs. "Nobody could find me. I was trapped under some debris. Dog stayed with me while everyone was running around camp preparing for a second strike. Tango knew he was putting himself in danger, you know? Stayed with me anyway. Then, when everything settled down, he ran off and found my commanding officer and led him right to me. I was obviously honorably discharged after I lost my legs. Tango got hurt during the air strike too. I don't know exactly what happened, but he's deaf in one ear now. Got a pretty bad limp, too, when the weather's no good."

"You told my friend here that your dog has PTSD?" Leo asked.

"Yeah. He was discharged right along with me because he couldn't do what he was trained to do after that," Elijah said. "You'd be amazed at all the paperwork I had to fill out to get Tango. I wanted to take care of him the way he did me. He's been trained as an emotional support animal. When I start to . . . start to get anxious . . . he picks up on it, you know? Calms me down . . . Aren't we some pair? Couple of marines with PTSD taking care of each other. You can't let them put Tango down. He wouldn't hurt anybody."

"But he did," Leo said. *And not just Jonathan,* he thought wryly. His leg twinged.

"But it wasn't his fault," Elijah said. "I know it wasn't. Someone took him out of my yard! If someone hadn't stolen him, no one would have gotten hurt!"

"How are you sure that someone stole him?" Mona asked.

"I got it on camera!" Elijah snapped, but he quickly calmed himself down. "Sorry, miss. I'm a little shaken, is all. Didn't mean to get upset with you."

"Let me see the footage," Leo said.

Elijah nodded. "Got to go back to my place."

"That's fine," Leo said. "I want to see it, and if it helps with the investigation, I'll see what I can do about Tango." His eyes softened, and he held Elijah's gaze. "I served overseas too. Our unit had dogs. I know what it's like over there."

Elijah seemed to visibly relax. "Thank you, sir."

"I'm coming with you," Mona said.

He glanced at her in silent question, but she didn't look directly at him. "Mona, please don't make this harder—"

She held up a hand. "I'm coming with you."

He shrugged, not wanting to fight about it in front of Elijah.

The three of them left the shop, and Mona locked up and joined Leo in the patrol car. He was painfully aware of her presence next to him, of her soft floral perfume, of the way her hair curled around her shoulders.

They followed Elijah a short distance away to a fairly isolated home in a new cul-de-sac.

Leo stepped out of the patrol car, eyeing the surveillance cameras in various places around the property.

Elijah climbed out of his own vehicle. "Footage is inside."

"Why all the cameras?" Leo asked.

"Some punks in the neighborhood kept setting off bottle rockets near my yard to scare Tango," he said, walking toward the door. "I wanted to catch them so I could show their parents. Tango is really jumpy. Can't blame him after what he's been through. He saw a lot more than I ever did. He was a marine dog long before I joined."

They headed inside, and Leo smiled at all the military paraphernalia. He would have been able to tell Elijah was an ex-marine just from the items in the room.

He could tell that this was a man who loved his country and was proud of his service to it. Elijah sat down at a desk and started up his computer. "This will just be a second," he said. He looked very anxious and fidgety. "You really think you could save my Tango?" He glanced back at Leo with sad eyes. "I know he's hurt someone . . . but . . . you don't think they'd make me put down a marine dog, do you? Not when his trauma was caused by active-duty service?"

"If we can figure out exactly what happened, we might be able to make a solid case for Tango," Leo said.

The computer finished booting, and Elijah took a moment to sift through some of the footage. "Tango was in the backyard that morning. A week ago today."

"So, last Monday?"

"Yes, sir."

The day Jonathan Darsey died.

"I went out for a run. I still work out." He tapped his prosthetic legs. "Running is actually a lot easier than walking with these things. Training for a triathlon."

"Impressive," Leo said.

"Okay, here it is. The video is a little fuzzy, but—"

It only took Leo a second to recognize the figure breaking into

Elijah's backyard and forcing a muzzle onto the poor dog. "That's Jonathan Darsey!"

"Who?" Elijah asked.

"The victim," Mona said. "The man Tango killed."

"See!" Elijah shouted. "See there? If that's him, that proves it! My dog must have just been defending himself, right? Right! He didn't do nothing any of us wouldn't have done; he was trying to get back to me!"

Leo wasn't so sure that any of them would have bitten a man in the throat, but Elijah certainly had a point. "Okay," he said slowly, "so Jonathan swiped Tango . . . but why?"

"Ugh, this is getting so confusing," Mona said. "We've got two dogs. One actually belonged to Jonathan, but Jonathan had Tango, not his own dog, Chippy. We also know that there was another person there because of the stab wounds on Jonathan and Chippy."

Leo rubbed his temples. "This is getting weirder and weirder. Why would Jonathan steal someone else's dog? You'd think he'd try to steal Chippy from Sharon, not take Tango. Had he given up and just wanted a new dog? But why not adopt one from the shelter like a normal person? And why did Chippy go missing too?"

"Who's Chippy?" Elijah asked.

"Jonathan's dog," said Leo. "A golden retriever who looks just like Tango. Jonathan's ex-wife got him in the divorce."

"Wait . . . what if . . ." Mona gasped aloud. "What if Jonathan took Tango *because* he looks just like Chippy?"

"What, to try to fill the void left by his old dog?" Elijah asked.

"No . . . not that . . ." Leo said, snapping his fingers.

He and Mona blurted in unison, "Jonathan was trying to swap the dogs!"

"He saw Tango and realized how much they looked alike," Mona continued. "There's no way he could have gotten away with stealing Chippy. If Chippy went missing, then everyone would know that Jonathan took him."

Leo nodded. "But Sharon wouldn't have even noticed that the dogs had been switched. She'd just think that Chippy was acting strangely all of a sudden."

"So." Mona stood and started pacing. "Jonathan followed whoever was walking Chippy—that's why he was in the woods! Whoever was walking Chippy out that way must have seen him. There was a confrontation, and he defended himself from Jonathan."

"He probably stabbed Jonathan," Leo said. "Jonathan screamed, scared Tango, and Tango bit him . . . then our killer stabbed Chippy? Maybe he couldn't tell them apart and just stabbed the nearest dog in the confusion."

"So, the question is: Who was walking Chippy?" Mona asked. "If we can figure that out, then . . ."

"Wait!" Leo snapped his fingers. "I know *exactly* who was walking Chippy."

CHAPTER 19

*L*eo's mind raced. He'd figured it out. He'd solved the case!

He glanced from Mona to the ex-marine. "Sharon told me her boyfriend's son takes Chippy for walks for her."

"Who's her boyfriend?" Mona asked.

"Nick Bonds," Leo said, gritting his teeth. "My so-called partner is friends with Nick's son . . ." Leo shook his head. "That's why Larry was at Nick's home before I got there. He was trying to find out if his buddy was the one who was with Jonathan when Tango killed him!"

"He was trying to keep his friend out of trouble," Mona said.

"So . . . who stabbed Jonathan and the other dog?" Elijah asked, confusion etched on his face.

"Albert Bonds," Leo said. "Nick Bonds's son. And I think my partner knows it!"

"You don't know that for sure, Leo," Mona said. "Talk to Larry first."

Jealousy welled in Leo's chest. "Don't worry—I'm not planning to arrest your new boyfriend without giving him a chance to explain himself."

Mona's jaw dropped, and hurt shone in her face. She grabbed her purse and strode to the door. "I'm calling a cab."

He followed her, already tasting regret. "Wait, I'm sorry. Don't do—"

She whirled on him. "Do. Not. Follow. Me." Then she stalked off, leaving Leo stunned in the hallway.

Elijah cleared his throat. "What about my dog? What about Tango?"

Leo took a deep breath and forced his thoughts back to the case. He put a hand on Elijah's shoulder. "I'll see what I can do. But Jonathan stole your dog, which this video proves. So it looks like we just might have a case to save Tango. The real criminal here seems to be our victim."

"This is crazy," Elijah said, shaking his head. "How could that guy have possibly thought something like this would work? I mean, switching the dogs?"

Leo shook his head. "I don't know. It was pretty far-fetched, but he tried it. Probably was hoping that Albert would let Chippy off his leash during their walk or something. Thought he could just swap them out. Probably didn't realize that you had cameras set up here, either."

"Can I go see Tango, please?" Elijah asked. "I just want to see him. Make sure he's okay."

"I'll take you to the morgue," Leo said. "The medical examiner is a friend of mine, and she's been keeping Tango. I can drop you off on my way."

"On your way where?" he asked.

Leo scrunched up his face. "On my way to talk to Larry Simmons."

* * *

LEO DROVE HIS CRUISER TOWARD THE BACK OF THE STATION'S PARKING lot and stepped out of the vehicle, leaning against the hood while he waited for Larry. In the meantime, he decided to pull out his laptop to research Albert Bonds. He sat on the hood of the car, setting the computer up in his lap. He started by typing the man's name into a search engine. The first thing that popped up was a story about a new pet store.

"What's this . . .?" Leo grumbled as he clicked the link.

There was a picture of a small shop in town. Leo recognized it but had never been inside. It was a pet shop for fancy dog supplies. He frowned when he saw the featured products—heinous bedazzled collars.

"So *that's* where Larry got that stupid collar for Chippy," he muttered.

Then he saw it—a promotion for dog-walking services. And, sure enough, there was a picture of Albert holding several dog leashes in a *very* familiar setting. He was standing at the trailhead for the Magnolia Falls Trail—the hike Leo and Mona had taken the day they found Jonathan's body.

"So, that's where you take your dogs for walks, eh, Albert?"

The story continued, mentioning that Albert had recently been released from prison. His mind raced.

Leo was certain. Albert had stabbed Jonathan. It was most likely self-defense, but he'd ditched Jonathan in the woods, leaving him to die alone. And, from the looks of it, Leo's partner had kept quiet about the whole thing.

He shot a text to Ann. *I need you to follow up on something for me right away. Is Albert Bonds still on parole?*

She replied, *I'll check. Is something wrong?*

He typed, *I'm about to meet Larry in the parking lot. I think—*

Larry whipped into the parking lot, so Leo just hit *send* without finishing the text.

His partner jumped out of his car as perkily as ever. "Hey, Leo!" he exclaimed. "Got your text to meet you here! You find anything on the Darsey case?"

"Yeah," Leo said, slamming his laptop closed and tossing it into his patrol car. He stood, arms crossed, as he stared Larry down.

"What's with the long face, Leo?" Larry asked. "Did I do something?"

"Albert Bonds," Leo said in a firm tone.

Larry paled.

"Tell me, how long have you known that your buddy Albert stabbed Darsey?"

Larry practically growled, "You seriously accusing my friend of something like that? Al wouldn't harm a fly, man."

"How long have you known?" Leo demanded again. "Covering something like this up . . . It's not right, Larry."

Larry looked like he was ready to sock Leo, so Leo squared his stance just in case this turned into a parking-lot brawl.

"How dare you! I'm a good cop, man!"

"Even if you didn't know," Leo spat, "even if you weren't covering it up, you knew more than you let on and decided to run off on your own and accuse everyone but your friend. You know how that looks."

"Besides"—Larry trained a harsh glare on him—"whoever stabbed Darsey didn't kill him. That damned dog did."

His phone buzzed. Ann had said, *Yes, Bonds is on parole. Are you OK?*

He didn't reply. He just looked back up at Larry. "You know, that's something that's always bothered me about this case. And it's something you've pointed out before. We have a nonfatal stabbing and a fatal dog bite. It looks to me like Bonds stabbed Darsey in self-defense."

"If he did," Larry said, "then he didn't commit a crime."

"Because even though it's a terrible thing to leave a man to die without reporting it, there's actually no law against it." Leo ran a hand through his hair.

"That's right." Larry looked defiant now.

"But Albert is on parole," Leo replied evenly.

Larry sucked in a sharp breath.

"Albert was Chippy's dog-walker," Leo said. "And Jonathan Darsey was the one who had the killer dog with him that day."

"What are you talking about?"

"The dog that killed Jonathan is an ex-military dog named Tango," Leo began. "I've got footage of Jonathan Darsey stealing the dog out of a disabled veteran's yard in the middle of the night. The dog has PTSD. It's why it freaked out and attacked me when it heard the loud music."

"So . . . why did this dog supposedly attack Jonathan?" Larry asked, crossing his arms.

"My guess is that when Albert let Chippy off the leash to go running around in the woods, Jonathan tried to switch the dogs. He wanted his dog back. Albert busted Jonathan making the switch and defended his charge with a knife. Jonathan probably started screaming, and it freaked Tango out," Leo said. "And, at some point during all of that, your friend stabbed Chippy too."

Larry kept shaking his head.

And then the last piece fell into place. Leo continued relentlessly, "Panicked, Albert called you from the scene of the crime, didn't he? He asked you what he should do. A man was dead, and Albert wasn't supposed to be carrying that knife. It was a violation of his parole. If he called the police, he'd go back to jail for a long time, even though he wasn't actually responsible for Darsey's death."

Larry's jaw dropped.

"You're a good friend," said Leo. "Loyal to a fault. You told him to leave the scene—to not even wait around to recover the dog—and to tell Sharon that he'd returned Chippy from the walk. Then you immediately requested a last-minute transfer back to Magnolia Falls and did everything you could to get on this case so that you could misdirect and protect your friend." His voice softened. "You were willing to give up your big-city career to help Albert. And there's something admirable about that. But it was still wrong. *Especially* for a police officer. Larry, can't you see that?"

Larry balled up his fists, and then his hand twitched toward his gun.

But a steely voice cut through the air. "I wouldn't do that, Simmons." Ann strode out from behind a police SUV, gun trained on Larry. "Larry Simmons, you're under arrest for obstruction of justice. Hands in the air."

Defeated, Larry raised his hands in surrender. Ann holstered her weapon and cuffed him.

"Good timing, partner," said Leo with a grin.

"I was worried when you didn't respond," she said, shoving Larry toward the station. "Thought I'd come out here and see what was up. Got here right in time to hear all the circus tricks that this clown has been up to. What do you say I take this guy in for processing and you go arrest Albert Bonds?"

Leo grinned. "It's a plan."

She swept a protesting Larry into the station, and Leo considered where he would be most likely to find Albert Bonds. The pet shop, he decided. His phone rang. It was Vicki again.

This time, he answered. "What is it?"

"Where are you?" she demanded.

He didn't have time for this. "Well," he said wryly, "I just arrested my partner for obstruction of justice, and now I'm on my way to arrest a suspect at the new pet shop."

"Wait, what? You arrested Ann? What did she *do*?"

"No, Larry Simmons. The chief stuck me with him on this case, remember?"

"Ooooh," she said softly. "Leo, you have to talk to Mona."

The words froze him in his tracks. "Vick, she doesn't want to date me. I'm sorry. I know you wanted it to work out, but it's over. I have to respect that."

"Listen—"

"I'm sorry, Vick. I've got to go. We'll talk tonight after I've made this arrest, all right?" He hung up over her words of protest and threw the car into gear.

When he arrived at the pet shop, he found himself cringing at the sheer gaudiness of it all. It was ridiculous; the collar Larry had bought for Chippy was actually *tame* compared to the rest of the store. Everything was goofy and bedazzled. There were even matching outfits for animals and people—all bedazzled!

"Oh, I just love it!" a familiar voice squealed.

Leo spun around to see Aunt Bee and Aunt Cee looking through racks of animal onesies.

"My little Noodles is going to look so cute in this!" Aunt Cee cried, pulling a bright-pink doggy tutu off the shelf.

Noodles? Leo smirked, spotting a white Pomeranian pup at Aunt Cee's side.

"Oh! Leo!" Aunt Bee spotted him, waving him over. "You must be here to get an outfit for Chippy!"

Leo scanned the store. Albert Bonds wasn't anywhere in sight. So he just smiled at the two elderly ladies. "Of course," he said, looking down at the Pomeranian. "And this is yours, Aunt Cee?"

"Oh, yes," Aunt Cee said. "My boyfriend gave her to me. Isn't she just the cutest? Bee told me all about this new shop, and I just had to stop by!"

Aunt Bee held up a sheaf of newspaper. "There was a coupon. I'm getting a Halloween costume for Vicki's duck. Don't you think Sunny will look so cute in this?" She showed him a yellow-and-black onesie that greatly resembled a bumblebee, and Leo chuckled.

Leave it to Aunt Bee to turn Sunny into one of his sister's bees for Halloween.

"Vick will love that," he said.

From the far side of the shop, a man called, "All right, ladies, I found the next size up in that bumblebee outfit!" Albert Bonds appeared around the corner, holding another one of the bedazzled bumblebee costumes. "This was originally designed for a larger kitten. I'm thinking it'll fit your friend's pet duck a little better."

"Perfect!" Aunt Bee cried, taking the collar from Albert. "I'm ready to check out."

"Oh, give me one more minute!" said Aunt Cee, still shuffling through the options.

"Of course." Albert smiled at Leo, but a momentary flicker of discomfort flashed across his face. "Hello, Officer. Can I help you find anything?"

"I need to speak to you about Jonathan Darsey," Leo said, not wasting any time.

"Sure. My Sharon's ex. What about him?" Albert said evenly.

"I think we'll just . . . go look back here at some of your gourmet dog treats while you two talk," Aunt Cee said, ushering Noodles toward the back of the shop. Aunt Bee followed, shooting Leo a questioning look.

Albert straightened nervously. "Um . . . so . . . what is it you need from me . . . Officer . . . ?"

"Detective Lawson," Leo said.

Albert instantly relaxed. "Oh! You're Larry's partner."

"That's right," Leo said. "I understand that you walked your father's fiancée's dog?"

"Yes—Chippy," he said. "Sharon told me you adopted Chippy. Are you here to stock up on stuff for him? Sweet dog. I'll be happy to sell you whatever you need at cost."

"When did Chippy go missing?" Leo asked.

"Oh, um . . ." His demeanor grew warier. "I don't remember exactly . . ."

"Does Sharon know you lost him on a walk? Or does she think he went missing in the middle of the night?"

Albert frowned. "What makes you think I lost him?"

"Oh, that's just what Larry told me you said," Leo lied.

Albert shifted. "Oh, well . . . um . . . yes," he said. "Sharon thinks he ran off in the middle of the night. I was too embarrassed to tell her that her dog got away from me."

"That's awfully dishonest of you," Leo said.

He cringed. "The woman's about to marry my old man. I didn't want her to know I lost her dog."

"Here's the thing, Albert—Larry didn't tell me that you lost the dog. He's already been arrested for obstruction of justice for helping you cover up what happened that day. So, why don't you go ahead and tell me exactly what happened when Jonathan Darsey tried to steal Chippy from you."

Albert froze. He looked like a deer in headlights. "Um . . . um . . . look, I didn't do anything! I didn't hurt anybody!"

"No, the dog did, right?" Leo asked. "But you stabbed the guy and one of the dogs with a knife that violated the terms of your parole. Then you called Larry for help and, at his advice, left Jonathan Darsey out in the middle of the woods to bleed to death. So, why don't you and I head down to the station where we can talk this whole thing through and—"

Albert abruptly headbutted him. Leo grunted, fumbling back into a shelf.

The bell above the door jangled, and Leo glanced wildly in that direction. Mona.

No.

Her eyes were misty, her hair mussed. A vision of angelic beauty. She gripped a cardigan tightly around herself. "Leo!" she called.

Leo lurched to his feet, but Albert had already reached Mona. He grabbed her around her shoulders and held a wicked-looking knife to her throat.

CHAPTER 20

*Mona stiffened, wide-eyed, as Albert tightened his grip on her.

Panic seized Leo's chest. He looked at the knife and held up a hand. "Albert, don't do anything stupid. We can work something out."

"Yeah," Albert said, "I think we can. You're going to stay here while the little lady and I get in my car and drive off. She'll be fine if you don't follow or call for help. I'll drop her off on the side of the road somewhere. But I'll be listening to the police scanner, so I'll know if you call it in."

"Hey, man," Leo said, grabbing his handcuffs from his belt. "Don't take her. Please." He clasped the cuffs on his own wrists. "Let her go. Take me." He held out his cuffed hands.

A tear ran down Mona's cheek.

Albert eyed Leo suspiciously. "Walk toward me slowly," he said.

When Leo reached them, Albert lowered the knife and shoved Mona away.

"Fine," he said. "I'll take you instead."

But Leo wasn't going down without a fight. He kicked Albert's hand, sending the knife clattering to the floor. Albert lunged at Leo, grabbed his arm, and twisted hard, sending Leo to his knees in pain.

Then Albert balled his fist as if to punch him in the face. But Leo jerked downward, throwing Albert off balance.

His assailant skidded back, seeming uncertain whether to fight or to run. In that moment of hesitation, Mona grabbed something off the counter and hurled it at Albert. The object flew through the air, smacking Albert in the back of the head. He swayed on his feet and fell to the ground, unconscious. Mona had whacked him over the head with a heavy dog bone.

"She got him!" Aunt Cee cried with a cackle.

Leo stood upright to see Aunt Bee hurrying toward them, gripping a dog leash. She and Mona moved to securely tie Albert's hands before he woke up. "Albert Bonds," muttered Leo. "You're under arrest."

When Albert was secure, Mona turned to Leo, her chin quivering.

"Hey," Leo said gently, "could you grab the key ring out of my pocket so we can get these cuffs unlocked?"

She nodded and assisted him out of the handcuffs. He breathed a sigh of relief when the cold metal clinked off his wrists, then he reached for his shoulder radio and called for an officer to assist at the pet shop.

"Thank you," he said to Mona. "I'm so glad you're safe. How . . . how did you know where I was?"

"Vicki told me. Leo—"

He held up his hands. "I want you to know that I respect your decision to end our relationship, Mona, but please don't go for Larry. He just tried to cover up a crime, and—"

"Leo!" she exclaimed. "My gosh, would you just *listen* to me?"

He bit his lip.

She continued, "I never *wanted* to just be friends. But if you were stuck being partners with Larry and . . . well, since it was bothering you so much that we'd been on a couple dates, I . . . I thought it'd be better to end it before it got too serious. So that it wouldn't be something that affected you at work."

It took a second for the full force of her words to sink in. "Wait, you don't have feelings for Larry?"

She snorted—an uncharacteristically unladylike sound. "No! I never have. Not even when we went on those dates."

"You weren't trying to defend him to me because you liked him?"

She shook her head. "I try to see the best in people. Larry's a more difficult case than most in that regard, if I'm being honest."

"Wait . . . so why did you date him?"

She let out a long sigh and glanced at Aunt Bee and Aunt Cee. "Don't tell my mom any of this," she said. "I don't want her to feel bad."

Aunt Cee clapped a hand over her mouth with a solemn nod, and Aunt Bee said, "Our lips are sealed."

Mona said, "I was kind of pressured by the family. Larry had asked me out a few times in the past, and I'd always turned him down because he just sort of gave off a weird vibe. Then he got his acceptance letter to Harvard, and my mom went nuts. Always mentioning me whenever she bumped into him, always talking him up to me. Mom wanted me to date him."

She hesitated, sweeping a hand through her beautiful hair. "He did everything right on paper, if that makes sense. Picked me up. Dressed up for the occasion. Opened the car door for me. Pulled out my chair when we went out to eat. But he was just so . . . annoying. Thought he was some big shot just because he got accepted to Harvard. Now, don't get me wrong, that was impressive. But it was like that was all he could talk about. He was a little creepy too. Whenever he complimented me, it felt . . . a little forced. And it was *always* physical. Like he thought the best thing about me was my looks. It was pretty clear he was just some self-proclaimed big shot who felt like he deserved an arm-candy girl, and that just wasn't and isn't me."

Relief swept over Leo, his knees going weak.

"Anyway," she continued, "it fizzled out when he went off to school, but that was more of a convenient excuse than anything. I wouldn't have continued dating him if he'd stuck around. I . . . I want to date *you*, Leo. I've cared about you for . . . years and years. Since we were kids. And I made such a big mistake when I pushed you away—" Her voice caught.

Leo didn't wait. He swept her into his arms and kissed her like he'd always wanted to kiss her, until the red-and-blue lights of a squad car interrupted them.

124

CHAPTER 21

*L*eo hopped out of bed. "Wake up, lazy bum!" he called, yanking the pillow out from under Chippy's head. The dog moaned, looking up at him with tired eyes. "Come on, don't give me that look. Today's a big day! I bet Vicki has some more honey treats ready for you . . ."

Chippy leaped out of bed, shaking off and stretching before prancing toward the door. Leo headed downstairs and let the dog run loose in the yard before making himself a quick breakfast. Today was a big day indeed! Today was Black Friday, and the grand opening of Mona's store, Jammin' Honey.

Finally.

Leo put a new—very plain—leash and collar on Chippy. He was so glad to be rid of the shimmering cop-themed collar. Then he dressed in a polo and jeans. He'd been sure to take the day off to help Mona and Vicki with the shop; launching on Black Friday was ambitious, and they were offering a lot of great deals while running a sort of celebration. They'd even brought in a little petting zoo to entice families.

"Come on, boy!" Leo called.

Chippy walked right alongside him, hopping up into the passenger's seat, his tail wagging.

"That leg of yours sure is looking a lot better," Leo said. The vet had removed Chippy's stitches, and the fur on his leg was already starting to grow back. He patted the dog's head as he pulled out of the driveway and headed into town, stopping first by the local florist shop. The bouquet he bought was much smaller than what Larry had sent Mona earlier, but he knew her well enough to know she wouldn't want anything big and showy. Just a few roses set in baby's breath. Something soft and subtle and romantic. However, he did spring for a vase so that Mona wouldn't have to figure out how to put the flowers in water.

The parking lot was packed with people. Children were petting goats and sheep, and there was even a bouncy castle. Much to Leo's amusement, he spied James—Vicki's boyfriend—in a clown costume making animal balloons. As Leo and Chippy marched up to him, Leo couldn't help but say, "James, *what* am I looking at?"

James laughed. "Vicki talked me into it. I let it slip to her that I knew how to do balloon animals, and she bought me the costume and promised me an unlimited supply of honey sticks in exchange for my embarrassment."

Leo snapped a picture with his phone. "Keeping it for blackmail."

"Don't you dare!" James exclaimed.

"Better treat my sister right! Hey, how's your mom doing?"

James's mom had been sick for a long time with Lyme disease, and Vicki had recently found a promising treatment for her—bee-venom therapy.

"The new treatment is working!" said James with a huge smile. "She's not back to normal yet, but we can see a difference. She has hope for the first time in a while."

"I'm so glad to hear that. Gotta find Vicki and Mona. I'll catch you in a bit, man." Smiling at the crowd, Leo headed toward the shop with Chippy.

Once inside, he spotted Vicki. She was explaining her body scrub flavors to a gaggle of enthusiastic teenagers. Once they made their choices and ran off toward the counter, Leo approached her.

"This looks amazing, Vick!" he exclaimed.

Her face shone. "Mona's put so much work into this. I'm so glad the store can finally open." Then she nudged him. "And I'm so glad the two of you are finally boyfriend and girlfriend for real. I *told* you that you needed to talk to her." She hid her face in her hands. "Imagine my distress when I realized the whole thing was a stupid misunderstanding. At least I persuaded her to go talk to you."

"At the shop where I was arresting a dangerous criminal," he deadpanned.

"In my defense," retorted Vicki, "I didn't expect you to be so darn slow about making that arrest. I figured the guy would definitely be in handcuffs before Mona walked in the door."

"Well, all's well that ends well," said Leo.

"Yup!" she said brightly. "Oh, and don't think you've gotten out of that double date. I've already rescheduled with Mona for next week."

He smiled. "Can't wait."

Two familiar voices called out in unison, "Fifteen percent off for the first fifteen customers who buy fifty dollars or more of jams and honeys!"

He looked up in time to see Aunt Bee and Aunt Cee strutting around in aprons that read *Jammin' Honey*. Aunt Bee was ringing a small bell as they announced the offer, and people scurried to grab as many jams and honeys as they could.

"They shout out a different deal every half hour," Vicki said. "I love how everyone brought their pets today."

"Oh?" Leo questioned.

"Elijah is here with Tango," she said, nodding toward the front of the shop. Then a group of customers came toward her, and she said, "Got to go. Customers await!"

Leo caught a glimpse of Elijah and Tango at the far end of the store. Tango was wearing a muzzle—he had to wear one in public until he could demonstrate a record of safe behavior—but Leo was just relieved the dog had avoided being put down. When the whole story came out—that Tango was a war hero with PTSD who had been stolen from his beloved human and had panicked when Jonathan and Albert were fighting over Chippy—public sentiment had turned decisively in his favor. They'd have had a riot on their hands if they'd tried to make Elijah put him to sleep.

Chippy whined nervously. "Oh, come on, he's not so bad, boy," Leo said, patting Chippy on the head. "Let's go say hello."

Chippy followed closely behind Leo as they approached the two former marines. "Leo!" Elijah called, stretching out his hand to shake. "I don't know how to thank you."

Chippy and Tango sniffed each other.

Leo knelt down, patting Tango on the head. "Good to see you too, Cujo."

Tango tried to lick Leo through the muzzle, as if to apologize for biting him.

"Leo!" Mona called, and Leo spun around to see her scurrying out of a back room. "So glad you're here! I could really use a hand!"

He bid farewell to Elijah and Tango and approached the counter, handing Mona the bouquet of flowers he'd gotten her.

"You are so sweet!" she said, leaning over to give him a kiss.

"I try," he said. "Chippy, sit tight for a second, okay, buddy?" He patted the dog on the head, and Chippy curled up behind the counter as Leo followed Mona to the back.

"I can't believe how busy it is!" she exclaimed.

"I can't believe Vicki convinced her boyfriend to dress up as a clown," Leo said, laughing.

"He sure is crazy about her."

"I sure am crazy about you," he said with a wink.

She shook her head, and he pulled her in for a long, lingering kiss. When they broke apart, Mona was breathless.

"Okay . . ." she said, her cheeks pink. "We're replacing some inventory that's running low out front. I need these three boxes taken out and shelved. You think you can handle that?"

"I think so," he said, picking up two boxes at a time. "These are the honey supplies, so they go on Vick's honeybee-themed shelf, right?"

"That's right!" she said happily and leaned in for one last hug. But Leo couldn't help himself. He turned his head, and their noses touched.

She grinned and went for it, giving him a kiss that made his stomach flip. Then she winked at him and shoved him toward the door. "Well, go on! Get those honeys out! They're going quick! I'm glad Vicki decided to make some extras for the grand opening! I think I'll change the music and be out in a second."

"On my way!" Leo said happily, heading out to the main floor of the shop.

Sheldon Goldberg was standing by the honeybee-themed shelves, sifting through the products.

"Heard you were breaking ground on your skating rink soon," Leo called.

"That's right!" Sheldon said. "You're going to come support me when I open up, right?"

"Of course," Leo said. "Although, I'm going to have to practice my skating first. Don't want to embarrass myself in front of my girlfriend."

Sheldon laughed. "I think it's just what this town needs."

"Absolutely," Leo said as Sheldon helped him place the honey products on the shelf.

The soft strains of "I Cross My Heart" reached Leo's ears, and his pulse pounded faster. This was *their* song now, wasn't it? He and Mona had a song.

He stopped and looked toward the counter. Mona came out from the back of the store and started ringing up customers at the second cashier's station. She and Leo locked eyes, and she gave him a soft smile. Leo finished stocking the shelf as George Strait's crooning voice hit the chorus for the second time. With his bin empty, he headed toward the counter just to be near Mona.

When he got there, Chippy stood up, tail wagging, a stray jar of jam in his mouth. He nudged his hand as if to urge Leo to take it.

Leo grinned and set the jar on the counter, and Chippy almost seemed to smile back at him. "Guess I'm gonna have to get used to the way you fetch everything," he said. "We're partners now. You'll never be lost again, boy."

LOOKING FOR SOMETHING NEW?

C heck out my other series Roundup Crew Available Now...

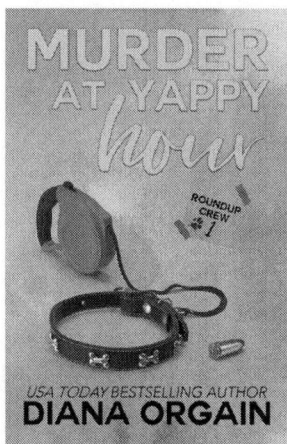

Click here to get your copy now.

PREVIEW OF YAPPY HOUR

CHAPTER 1

"What do you mean, you fired her?" I said into my cell phone as I brushed sand from the beach towel.

It was at least the fourth time I'd had the same conversation with my great-uncle Ernest. Grunkly-E we called him, which morphed into Grunkly, but on occasion turned into Grouchy or Grumpy. He was one of the reasons I'd recently relocated to Pacific Cove. He and my sister, Rachel, not to mention the fact that my stint as a financial advisor in New York had come to an abrupt end after the market had crashed.

It was time to hit the reset button on my life. What I needed most was some fresh seaside air, and when I'd learned that the Soleado Mexican Riviera Cruise Line had opened a new port in town, the position of bookkeeper/purser practically shouted out my name.

"Well, Maggie, she was real mean. She wanted me to walk around and stuff," Grunkly said.

A few months back, Grunkly suffered a mild heart attack. He'd been hospitalized and on the verge of "the great beyond" as he called it, but he'd battled back from the heart attack and the case of pneumonia he'd contracted. Actually, at his age of eighty-four, the doctors all considered it a miraculous recovery. Now our biggest obstacle was finding him a day nurse that he liked, or rather, wouldn't fire at the drop of a hat.

"You're supposed to walk around! Breathe some fresh air. That's how you're going to get better."

"I'm already better. Plus, she didn't like Benny. Actually told him I wasn't home, when I was."

I laughed. Benny was Grunkly's longtime bookie. If anyone got in the way of Grunkly's gambling they were sure to get the ax.

"I wanted to place a bet on Winged Arrow. The odds are seven to two. Is he there now?" Grunkly asked.

"Here? I'm at the beach," I said.

"I know the trainer, Aaron, was going to take Winged Arrow out there, to walk in the salt water. It's good for the hooves. I thought maybe Benny might be with them."

I glanced up and down the beach. There was a couple near me perched on a plaid blanket, a platinum blonde who looked like an escapee from *America's Next Top Model* with her Ken-doll boyfriend. Then in the distance was a group of people walking their small dogs.

I figured the group had to be the Roundup Crew, or at least part of them. I knew from my sister, Rachel, that this group met every Friday on the beach for a walk that ultimately ended up at her bar, The Wine and Bark, for Yappy Hour. My sister was as happy-go-lucky as they came, and I was glad she found her calling running a bar; it seemed the perfect fit for her personality.

"No, Grunkly. I don't see Benny or Aaron and Winged Arrow."

"That's too bad." He paused. There was a small sound as if he was lighting a cigarette.

"You're not smoking, are you?"

Grunkly had smoked for over sixty years.

"No," he said, almost too fast. "I'm not supposed to be smoking, Magpie!"

"I know you're not *supposed* to be smoking! But it kind of sounded like you just lit a cigarette."

"No," he said again.

"So, what I'm figuring is that the nurse who came over today wasn't letting you smoke and—"

"Sweetheart," he said quickly. "I'm wondering if I could bother you to run an errand for me."

I smiled to myself. He'd do anything to get me off the topic of his smoking.

"What errand? I'm not buying you a carton of Lucky Strikes," I said.

A seagull landed on my towel and thrust its beak out at me, accusingly. No doubt looking for crumbs. I pulled a roll of Ritz Crackers out of my bag, the motion scaring the bird away.

"I was thinking you could pick me up a nice cut of steak. Go to the Meat and Greet. They always have some nice filet mignons on hand."

The Meat and Greet was a locally owned shop that sold quality cuts of meat and hand-painted greeting cards. The downturn in the economy had hit Pacific Cove so hard that it seemed almost every shop or storefront did double billing just to stay in business. There was Bradford and Blahnik—which was a law firm selling designer shoes in order to keep their practice open. Dreamery Creamery, the ice cream shop that sold kids' clothes, and Magic Read, which was part magic shop and part bookstore/café.

Even Rachel was running a semi-double business with a wine bar that catered to dog owners and their beloved beasts.

"Sure, there's nothing I wouldn't do for my Grunkly," I said, breaking up a cracker and dropping the bits on the sand next to my towel. The seagull returned followed by a flock of its friends. I crumbed the rest of the package and stood. It was getting too hot to sit at the beach, anyway. Sweat was dripping down my face. I needed some shade. "I'll pick up a couple of steaks and be over later."

<><><>

AFTER DROPPING MY BEACH BAG AT MY APARTMENT AND TAKING A QUICK shower, I frantically checked messages. There was no update from the

Soleado Cruise Line. Well, after all, it was late Friday afternoon. I couldn't be too disappointed.

Didn't most hiring managers reach out early in the week?

Yes, Monday I would surely get a call to schedule an interview. I just had to stay optimistic, and there was nothing like shopping to keep one's spirits up. I slipped my credit card into my jeans pocket and headed downtown.

It was a short walk on a small cobblestone path. The town should have been called Pacific Charm, because that's exactly what it exuded. There was a fountain in the center of the town square with a marble statue of a man on a horse. It was rumored that the statue was of the town's founder, yet the placard had mysteriously disappeared ages ago, and nobody I talked to could remember the founder's name. The statue looked remarkably like John Wayne. The only way I could reconcile this in my mind was that either the Duke had founded Pacific Cove or the artist who had created the statue had been a fan.

The town square was flanked by restaurants and little shops. In one corner of the square was a sundial and opposite that was Rachel's bar. I glanced at my watch. It was early, still only 4:00 p.m., but Rachel might already be there prepping for Yappy Hour. I decided to pop in on her after picking up the steaks for Grunkly. From another corner, the smell of homemade waffle cones wafted through the air.

Ah, the Dreamery Creamery!

First the steaks, then I'll splurge on a cone before dropping in on Rachel.

I stopped in front of the window of Designer Duds. There was a handbag in the shape of a chicken prominently displayed. I stifled a giggle. The jacket on the mannequin next to the chicken bag, however, was what caught my eye. It was navy blue with little white anchors embroidered on it. I imagined showing up to an interview with Soleado Cruise Line wearing the jacket.

Too overzealous?

Probably.

I walked on toward the Meat and Greet and entered the small butcher shop, a bell going off as I stepped on the welcome mat.

A voice called out from the back. "I'll be right with you."

"No problem," I called back, marveling at the selection on display.

There was a large butcher counter filled with prime cuts, and in front of the counter was a delectable-looking collection of gourmet cheeses and chutneys.

I noticed a small rack of greeting cards and picked one up. It was a hand-painted watercolor rendition of the beach. Another was a watercolor version of the town square. The sundial was depicted in various cards. Some cards were of parts of the cove itself that I had yet to visit, but most were studies of sea creatures. My favorites were a close-up of a starfish, and another of a jellyfish, its luminescent colors splashed across the card. They were all done by the same artist, someone named Coral.

Something stirred inside me. Years ago, when life was simple, I'd loved to paint. I probably was never as gifted or dedicated as Coral — whoever she was—but maybe it would be a nice pastime again. Life had been so busy in New York that I'd felt I'd almost lost myself; maybe painting would help me put some pieces back together.

"Thanks for waiting." A middle-age woman in a butchers coat appeared from the back of the shop and hustled to her place behind the counter. She had unruly dark hair and dimples when she smiled, making me smile back at her.

"No worries," I said. "I just came in for a cut of meat for my uncle."

The woman studied me a moment. "Your uncle? Who's that? I know everyone in town and I don't think we've met yet."

"My great-uncle Ernest—"

"Oh! Are you Maggie? Ernest has told me so much about you! His little Magpie. He is so proud of you, and of Rachel, too. Well, the whole town is proud of Rachel. What a doll, an absolute doll. How do you like Pacific Cove?"

"Just getting settled in—"

"Yes, it takes some time. Are you staying at the Casa Ensenada Apartments? *Ensenada* means *cove* in Spanish, did you know? Those little apartments are so charming. Do you have one with a little patio and ocean view?"

I laughed. After living in New York City for a stint, it seemed unreal that a perfect stranger would not only know where I was living, but actually know the layout of my apartment. "I do have an ocean view."

The woman smiled. "Lovely. Lovely. You'll have to have a house-warming! We could do something fun," the woman continued. "Like a stock-the-bar party." She wiggled her eyebrows at me.

"If I manage to get hired at Soleado, I'll schedule a party immediately," I said.

"Oh! Have you applied to the new cruise line?" she asked. "Yeah. Bookkeeper, but I guess in ship lingo its called purser."

"Right. I hear you're a financial whiz!" she said.

"I don't know about that—"

The woman laughed, a low deep satisfied rumble that would make anyone in earshot vibrate. "You're just being modest! Rachel raves about you. You should have her put in a word for you. They need someone sharp. You have to deal with foreign currency and whatnot. Now what can I get for you? Is Ernest feeling any better? We had such a scare a few weeks ago. Is his appetite back?"

"He's requesting a filet, so I think we can safely say he's on the road to recovery."

The woman took a tray of meat from behind the counter and placed a few cuts onto butcher paper. "I know he likes the marbled ones. How many filets?"

"Two," I said.

I hadn't officially been invited to dinner, but I suspected Grunkly would want me to stay. Besides, I didn't have any other plans except to hover over my phone waiting for a call from the cruise line. It'd be good to get my mind off it for a while.

The woman wrapped up the meat and placed it into a pink plastic bag. I paid and headed out into the bright sunlight, a cool ocean breeze sweeping over my face. Thankfully the heat of the day was finally relenting a bit.

My phone buzzed.

Soleado!

I pulled my phone from my pocket and glanced at the screen. It was a text from Rachel.

· · ·

MAGGIE, I'M GOING OUT OF TOWN UNEXPECTEDLY. I KNOW IT'S SHORT notice, but can you tend to The Wine and Bark until I get back? Yappy hour is at 5pm. You have a key, don't you? If not, ask Dan, the manager at DelVecchio's. xoxox

HOW STRANGE. THIS WASN'T LIKE RACHEL AT ALL.

She was going out of town? Where?

Why hadn't she said anything about it to me earlier? While I had no problem helping out my sister, I hesitated over dealing with the dogs, as they never seemed particularly friendly to me.

I checked my watch; it was almost four thirty now. I fumbled with my phone and dialed her number. I did have a key for the bar on me, but something in my gut began to buzz with worry.

Her voice mail clicked on.

I left a quick message, "Hey Rach, what's going on? I'm on my way to the bar now. Hope you're okay. Call me." I made my way across the cobblestone walkway toward The Wine and Bark. I dialed Grunkly next. He picked up on the first ring.

"Hi, Grunkly, I got a message from Rachel. She needs me to cover for her at the bar."

"Oh, uh huh."

It was his distracted voice. "Grunkly, are you watching a race?"

"No, it's ten minutes to post," he said.

That explained it.

"Have you seen Benny?" he asked.

I laughed. "Well, I didn't run into him at the Meat and Greet."

"Uh huh," Grunkly said.

"I got your steak, though."

"Great," he said.

"But I have to go to The Wine and Bark—"

"No problem, honey. I'll have a can of Dinty Moore stew."

"All right. Should I save the steaks for tomorrow?"

"That'd be really nice," Grunkly said with such a flat tone that I knew he wasn't listening to a word I said.

Nevertheless, I insisted on asking, "Do you know where Rachel is?"

"Oh, Magpie, I got a call beeping in. I have to get it. It could be Benny."

Before I could say anything else, Grunkly hung up on me.

I sighed as I stood in front of the antique wooden door of The Wine and Bark. It was painted blue and orange and had a "happy vibe" practically pulsing right through it. I had to give Rachel credit, she'd built the place from the ground up with limited funds and now the business was thriving.

I laced the pink plastic bag around my wrist, then dug for the key in my pocket. When I shoved the key into the lock, the first thing that struck me was that I hadn't needed the key after all. The door wasn't even locked.

Now that really isn't like Rachel.

The hair on the back of my neck stood up. I pushed open the door and stepped into the darkened bar. My eyes adjusted slowly, the outline of the great L-shaped mahogany bar coming into view, then a few tables with stools perched on top to facilitate mopping the floors, and then near the back of the bar, right in front of the small corridor that led to his and hers, the silhouette of a woman standing over a body slumped on the floor.

Rachel, what have you got me into?

TO CONTINUE READING...

*C*lick here to purchase now...

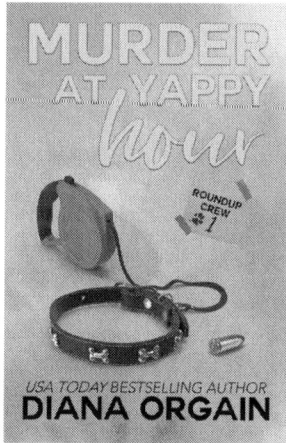

Click here to get your copy now.

OTHER TITLES BY DIANA ORGAIN

Third Time's a Crime If only love were as simple as murder…

ROUNDUP CREW MYSTERY SERIES

Yappy Hour Things take a *ruff* turn at the Wine & Bark when Maggie Patterson takes charge

Trigger Yappy Salmonella poisoning strikes at the Wine & Bark.

iWITCH MYSTERY SERIES

A Witch Called Wanda Can a witch solve a murder mystery?

I Wanda put a spell on you When Wanda is kidnapped, Maeve might need a little magic.

Brewing up Murder A witch, a murder, a dog…no, wait…a man..no…two men, three witches and a cat?

COOKING UP MURDER MYSTERY SERIES

Murder as Sticky as Jam Mona and Vicki are ready for the grand opening of Jammin' Honey until…their store goes up in smoke…

GET SELECT DIANA ORGAIN TITLES FOR FREE

$$\mathcal{B}$$

uilding a relationship with my readers is one the things I enjoy best. I occasionally send out messages about new releases, special offers, discount codes and other bits of news relating to my various series.

And for a limited time, I'll send you copy of BUNDLE OF TROU-BLE: Book 1 in the MATERNAL INSTINCTS MYSTERY SERIES.

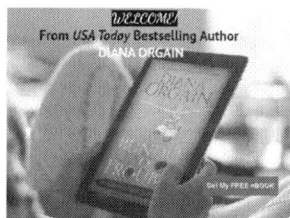

Join now

ABOUT THE AUTHOR

*D*iana Orgain is the bestselling author of the *Maternal Instincts Mystery Series*, the *Love or Money Mystery Series*, and the *Roundup Crew Mysteries*. She is the co-author of NY Times Bestselling *Scrapbooking Mystery Series* with Laura Childs. For a complete listing of books, as well as excerpts and contests, and to connect with Diana:

Visit Diana's website at www.dianaorgain.com.

Join Diana reader club and newsletter and get Free books here